The Shaun Hupp Collection Volume 1

Shaun Hupp

Cover design by Shaun Hupp

<u>Acknowledgements</u>

They say it takes a village to raise a child. The same can be said about a book. Most people just see my name on the cover. They don't know about the people in the background, behind the scenes. Without that help, this book simply would not have been born. It is an evolution of creativity and I owe many people thanks for their contributions.

To name a few;

W.B. Grape and Dottie Turner edited and proofread most of these stories and for that, I am eternally grateful. You guys kicked my butt grammatically. Also, much love goes out to my beta readers for helping me to articulate my stories, for you, my audience. Their opinions helped me fill plot holes with dead bodies and their suggestions covered those same holes with dirt so nobody would notice. They are my accomplices.

I'd like to give a special mention to author Matt Shaw for all his advice and support. He took a gamble with his own reputation as a successful writer to include me, along with other emerging writers in a collection to promote my writing career. Goodwill is rare, and it will be reciprocated. I am truly proud to have gone from being a fan to his colleague and friend. Just don't tell him I said that.

Finally, I'd like to give a special thank you to Christina Cooper over at Fans of Modern Horror. Her genuine love of the written word and her relentless push and promotion of my work has left me truly humbled. Christina, you have slightly warmed my cold, dead heart. You should feel proud. Keep doing what you're doing and I'll keep on writing.

Shaun Hupp

Shaun Hupp

CONTENTS

MOTHER

The old man sat alone and that's the way he liked it. He wasn't a people person, but he could if need be. And now it need be. He suddenly felt so weak. He didn't understand why he let himself get like this. It wasn't like it was getting harder. People were easily distracted by their cell phones, Kindles, and other varies technologies he himself didn't understand. And those that weren't blinded by their handheld devices were out causing chaos he so yearned for. Bloodshed. Mayhem. He wasn't a picky man. He needed it while the others watched through the protection of their digital screens. No. This should be easy.

He needed an outlet to charge his batteries, but as he sat in his uncomfortable seat, inside this dirty rectangle, flying along the tracks down a tube underneath the city of New York, he realized that he might just die in that seat, turning this subway car into his coffin.

I must feed. Now.

"Mom, would you listen to me for once? Me and Ryan are going City University."

The old man's attention perked. No one else was talking in this subway car. He was about to move on, but this had potential. Perhaps he might make it a few more days.

"Marianne, you've got good grades. You can really go places. You can do much better than City University."

"Don't you mean 'better than Ryan'?"

"No. I didn't mean-"

"You know what, Mother? Maybe, you're right. Maybe WE shouldn't go there. Maybe WE should both go somewhere far away from here and far away from you!"

The teenage left her seat and moved towards the front of the train car. She sat next to a young man about her age and wrapped her arms around him. The old man assumed that he must be one they were fussing about. She put in a pair of earbuds and curled up in his arms, while her mother sat fuming.

The other passengers turned away and looked out the window to either ease her embarrassment or theirs. This made it so much simpler for the old man. He stood as quick as his aching bones would allow and made his move. His cane thumped against the floor of the subway car, but it was easily masked by the sounds of the rails. The mother didn't even see him until he sat down next to her in the seat that was previously her daughters.

She jumped. "My GOD! You scared me."

He smiled. "No. I most definitely am not God. My name is Emrys Sarlic and I did not mean to frighten you."

Emrys put out his ancient hand. She reluctantly took it. "Joan."

"Ahh, such a beautiful name for such a beautiful woman. I couldn't help but hear you and your daughter."

"I'm sorry. I didn't mean to disturb anybody. It seems like we've been having this same fight over and over. We just can't-"

Emrys raised his cane up so the top was eye level and Joan couldn't seem to find her voice. The cane figured a white glass globe with just a little bit of red at the bottom. The insides seemed to swirl, memorizing Joan.

"Love and college. Both are counterproductive to each other bur regardless, they always happen. However, this doesn't mean you should let this go. The combination of the two can prove very dangerous, deadly even."

Joan was unmoving. The rest of the train car didn't seem to even notice the two of them anymore as if they were in some kind of blind spot.

"I want to tell you a story, if I may? It's not a happy story I warn you, but a necessary one. It's a story of revenge and love gone wrong. It's a story that could very well be your daughter's if you let it."

Joan slowly nodded, watching the swirling white within the globe dance. She was no longer riding the subway. She was within his words as he began his tale.

I WILL
MAKE YOU
LOVE ME

Shaun Hupp

Megan Weber reluctantly opened her mouth and let him put it in. There was no use refusing or trying to get away. Her hands were bound together with multiple layers of thick duct tape behind her back. He had forced her to her knees and his grip on her long, black hair would only tighten if she struggled. Within seconds, the long shaft was sliding in and out between her pouty but unwilling lips.

"Suck it. Suck it like you used to."

She looked up and met Nick's eyes. She could barely see them through his shaggy, brown hair. He normally kept his hair professionally trimmed short, but he obviously didn't care anymore. She silently pleaded him not to do this, but those dark eyes were not the same baby blue eyes she fell in love with. Those eyes were gone. That man was gone. She lowered her gaze back to the task at hand and did as he said.

"You fucking like that, don't you? Do you miss it?"

Megan couldn't speak. She tried to nod her head as Nick's thrusts intensified. She gagged as he struck the back of her throat. He wasn't this rough when they were a couple. She had never seen this side of him.

"That's a good girl. Bet you wish it was the

real thing."

Nick pulled the six-inch barrel of his Smith and Wesson revolver out of her mouth. Its front sight knocked against her top teeth as it exited. Nick's right hand was firmly around the wooden grip as he aimed the weapon between her eyes. Her saliva dripped off its black finish.

"Please," she begged. "You don't have to do this."

Nick laughed. "What choice do I have? You dumped me. You called me a *mistake*. Well, this *mistake* is going to set things right."

Megan sobbed uncontrollably while the man she once loved held a gun to her forehead. Why was he doing this, she asked herself. She had broken up with him about a year ago, but she had told Nick that she wanted to remain friends. He agreed, however quickly disappeared. No texts. No calls. He even left his job. She hadn't seen him since. She thought this part of her life was over and done with. She was happy now in her new relationship. She had moved on. Apparently, Nick did not.

"I told you... I can't change who I am."

Nick pistol whipped the side of her head and without the use of her hands, Megan hit the floor hard on her side. At that moment, she was glad she finally finished renovating the inside of this old farmhouse after her parents left it to her. She had replaced the roof, fixed all the windows, painted all the walls, and most importantly, installed carpeting. Even so, she saw stars and before she could sit up, Nick flipped her over and pushed her face against the floor. She could feel his muscular frame pushing down on her tiny torso and more worrisome, the barrel pressed against the back of her head.

"Well, go on. You're a carpet-muncher now, right?"

Crude, but he was right, she thought. Over a year ago, she finally realized she was a lesbian. While she cared a great deal for Nick, she never fully felt comfortable with him or any other guy in that way. It was hard to explain, but she knew she wasn't feeling the same things that other girls felt with their boyfriends. It was as if she was playing some part in a play. She was trying to be the person her friends and family wanted her to be. After so many failed relationships with men her age, she had thought that maybe dating an older man was what she needed. None of her friends approved of Nick. One of her friends even suggested that she was trying to replace her father with him. She pressed on hoping that those feelings would bloom inside of her.

They never did.

As she grew more and more depressed, she sought out comfort in a fellow student she didn't know very well. She thought the girl was just friendly. It turned out that she was attracted to Megan. After a drunken night of experiences Megan never had before, she knew, then and there, who she was. She couldn't even remember the girl's name, but she will never forget the way she made Megan feel. It was as if the final piece of the puzzle was put into place and she could finally be happy with whom she was as a person.

When she met Nick for dinner the next night, she had planned to tell him about her revelation and break up with him. She hoped he would take it well. I'm just a college student, she thought. I shouldn't be expecting anything serious out of him and neither should he. We're just two people having a good time.

Nick had different plans that night.

He had a ring in his pocket.

"You said you loved me!" he screamed, shocking her back to present-day reality. "I left my wife for you. I risked my whole career for you."

He was right again. They had met as student and teacher at a state university. She was in her first year, trying to finish up her prerequisites when she decided to take Professor Heston's Intro to American History class. She was barely passing her other classes, but she excelled in his class. Professor Heston showed such passion during his lectures that she hung on every word. She quickly found herself moving from the back of the lecture hall to the front row, from the classroom to his office, from calling him Professor Heston to calling him Nick, from campus coffee shops to hotel rooms. Before she knew it, she was in a full-fledged relationship with a man twenty years her senior, and he was leaving his wife for her.

"I'm sorry, Nick. I truly am. I didn't mean for any of this to happen. I had just moved out of my mom's house and started college. Everything was so new to me. I didn't even know myself."

"It's too late to apologize. What's done is done, but don't you worry. I can fix this."

Nick climbed off her and rolled her onto her back. He reached into his pocket and pulled out a grey rag. He used it to wipe the spit off his gun. Megan could smell the oil on the cloth.

It was then that she remembered what had

happened. It all came rushing back to her. There was a knock on the door. She wasn't expecting anybody and didn't receive many visitors this far out in the country. She could see a shadowy silhouette behind the frosted glass window on the almost new door. She didn't even think twice before she opened it. She was so shocked to see Nick standing there. His unkempt hair, unshaven face, and clothes were so out of character for him. In the past, he had always liked to dress professionally, whether he was in the classroom or lounging around at home. His closet had nothing but sweater vests and tweed jackets. He stood at the entryway in an old, stained sweatshirt and torn jeans that looked like they weren't good enough for the Goodwill. No words were shared between them. Her jaw hung open and she didn't have time to react, as he lunged for her and pressed that smelly rag over her mouth and nose. When she awoke, she found herself staring down the barrel of one of the guns from his antique collection.

The present situation hadn't changed much.

"You see, Meg, while you were snoozing, I did some snooping. I've been watching you for some time now and I know what your girlfriend looks like, but I didn't know her name. Luckily, all you kids have cell phones and you didn't delete those text messages from earlier today. You know the ones. *I love you more. No, I love you more.* Guess what, darling? I texted Shannon and she should be here any minute."

Megan felt her heart stop. "Don't hurt her!"

Nick smiled and started walking in a circle around her. "That's exactly what I plan to do, Meg. That's part one: Kill the bitch. Do you want to know what part two is? I bet you can't guess."

"Please...I'll do whatever you want. Just leave her alone."

Nick brought his boot down on the side of her ribs. Megan curled up in the fetal position with tears streaming down her face.

"You were supposed to say, *'Why yes, Nick. I would love to hear part two of your brilliant plan.'* And I would say, 'Thank you for asking and being so polite, Meg'.

Part two involves the concept of Stockholm's Syndrome. Pop quiz time, class. Have you heard of it? Probably not. Too busy making googly eyes at your teacher and ruining his life. Anyways, the year was 1973. In Stockholm, Sweden, some bank employees were taken hostage for about six days, around 130 hours. In that short amount of time, they formed an emotional connection to their captors to the point of sympathizing with them and even defending them after they were free.

That's what I want from you, darling. I'm not going to kill you. I just want to keep you here for a while. We'll talk and reminisce about the good times. Eventually, you will start falling for me all over again. I want you to love me again. I WILL make you love me. Say that you love me."

"I . . . I can't."

Nick brought his foot down, stomping on her ribs again. "Say it!"

"I . . . HATE YOU!"

Nick had his foot raised for another assault but put it down. Instead, he climbed on top of Megan and wrapped his hands around her throat. "It doesn't have to be like this, Meg. Why are you being so difficult? It can be like it was. What do I have to do? Brick up all the windows and doors? I'll do it if it means you'll love me again."

Megan tried bucking him off with her legs and hips, but it was no use. He outweighed her and with her hands behind her back, she had no chance of prying his off her neck. She couldn't get any air and was fading fast. The last thing she had heard before she passed out was Nick whispering in her ear, "I love you."

Megan felt like everyone in the restaurant was staring at them. Friday night was date night in Anytown, USA. Every table in this fancy restaurant had two people: One man and one woman. That is, except for theirs.

"Hello? Earth to Meg."

Megan turned her attention back to her date, Shannon. She was tall, blonde, and very attractive. She would be Megan's type if Megan had dated the same sex long enough to even have a type. And from the way each of them dressed in those short, tight, black dresses, nobody in the room would confuse them for sisters eating out.

"I'm listening. It's just that I'm not used to this. I don't think I've been out on a *date*-date with a woman before."

"Oh, I'm sorry. Is picking up straight, drunken sorority girls more your thing, I take it?"

Megan blushed and looked away. It was true. Ever since she'd found out she was gay, she started going to a lot of parties, finding the drunkest, hottest girls, and seeing how far she could take things. Sometimes they ended up back at her apartment, but most of the time, it was just some random room at whatever frat or sorority house where the party was being held. Almost all of the women were straight, but Megan didn't care as long as she got what she wanted. She wasn't interested in jumping into another long term relationship since she just broke up with what's-his-face.

Shannon was different, though. Shannon was in her Composition class at the University. They had to work together on an assignment for a few weeks. Megan was attracted to her, but unless she planned on sneaking alcohol into the classroom, it wasn't going to happen. To her surprise, Shannon made the first move and asked her out on a date.

"I'm new to all this," admitted Megan. "I guess I don't have a very good 'gaydar' or whatever you called it. If I can't spot them, how can I ask them out? I'm not used to being *out* in public either. It feels weird."

Shannon smirked. She picked up her butter knife and water glass. She struck the glass several times, silencing the room. "May I have your attention, please?"

"What are you doing?"

Shannon shushed her and went back to addressing the room, "I'd like to make an announcement. We're lesbians and we're on a date. That is all."

Shannon put down her glass, grabbed a dinner roll, and used the knife to butter it. All the while, Megan wanted to die right there. The restaurant sat in stunned silence and then, gradually, returned to normal.

"Feel better?" Shannon had asked before she took a bite.

"Not really. I can't believe you did that. What are you going to do on our next date? Buy a billboard with a picture of the two of us?"

Shannon smiled. "Why, Meg, did you just ask me out on a second date? I do believe I've made some progress with you. Billboard? Usually, lesbians bring moving trucks with them to their second dates."

Megan gave her a weird look.

"Sorry. Bad lesbian joke. Yes, Meg, if you're asking, I'd love to go out on another date with you, but I'd really like to finish this one first."

Their plates arrived and left with no more embarrassing incidents. The two walked out of the restaurant after some flirtatious small talk. Oddly enough, Megan did find herself more comfortable after Shannon told everyone in the room her 'dirty secret'. After eating, they went to a local bar that Megan knew all too well. Shannon promised she wasn't going to get drunk. She didn't want Megan taking advantage of her on the first date. They were going to take it slow. Maybe on the second date, she joked, they could do it in the back of the moving truck.

But once again, Shannon made the first move. Kissing led to heavy petting, which led to cheers and leers from the bar patrons. It was Shannon who suggested taking it back to her dorm for some privacy.

They walked hand-in-hand to the ironic 'girls only' dorm. They rushed to her room as fast as they could to avoid the monitors. Once there, the kissing and groping resumed. They fell onto the bed together with Shannon on top. Shannon's mouth tasted of strawberries, like the daiquiri she was drinking.

Shannon's lips left hers. She took Megan's hands off her breasts and forced them against the bed. Megan was confused until she saw Shannon's smirk. Shannon sat up, climbed on top of her, and asked Megan to close her eyes. When she did, Megan felt her dress being pulled up above her hips. Megan shuttered as Shannon's hand pressed against her stomach and slowly slid down the front of her black, silk thong. Her fingers brushed passed her trimmed pubic hair and two slid inside her wetness.

Megan arched her back and moaned. As she

gripped the sheets, she opened her eyes and was staring directly into Shannon's. Her lips trembled as Shannon's fingers moved faster. This is the one, she thought. No more taking home straight girls in the hopes of making a connection. This was real. This was what she really wanted.

Megan wanted to touch Shannon, but her hands still gripped the sheets, unable to move. Their eyes were still locked. She felt an orgasm coming as Shannon's fingers teased and thrust into her. Shannon closed her eyes, breaking eye contact, and leaned down. Meg closed her eyes too and her lips parted as Shannon's tongue found its way in. Megan was on the verge of screaming in pleasure.

But something was wrong. The sweet flavor of strawberries was gone and in its place, the taste of cheap whiskey. Megan's eyes flashed open.

Nick was on top of her.

She felt his coarse face against hers and his tongue swirling around in her mouth. Even worse, she could feel that her jeans were undone and his hand was inside her underwear. She was repulsed and felt bile coming up the back of her throat. Without thinking, Megan bit down hard on his tongue. Nick let out a yell and pulled himself away. She no longer had to worry about tasting whiskey. The coppery taste of blood filled her mouth now.

"Fucking bitch!" Nick screamed as he brought his foot down repeatedly on her already sore ribs. Megan was crying in pain, but also because of the violation. She curled up onto her side and prayed to God for help or to just to let her die right there. All of a sudden, the blows stopped and Nick walked over to the window.

Megan wiped her eyes on the carpet the best she could. She looked down at her open jeans and her lace panties, Shannon's favorite. That's when she saw it: A nail file. She had been looking for it a couple of days ago and there it was, under an end table. It was only a couple of feet away from her. She quickly looked away and back at Nick, hoping he didn't see what she saw.

He was too busy looking out the window. "I think we have company."

Megan knew it was Shannon. She could now hear the distinct sound of a car with a broken muffler. It was damaged weeks ago when she was driving down the dirt road to Megan's house. As a poor college student, she had little money for car repairs and it would have to wait until a student loan kicked in. Megan was so used to the sound that she could tell that Shannon was at the end of her long, private driveway.

Megan knew she had to act quickly. While Nick was distracted, Megan had to take this opportunity to quickly and quietly roll over to the nail file. She got on her stomach and rolled onto her back. Almost there, she thought. She rolled onto her stomach again and then, to her back. She heard a crack and bit down on her lip to stop from screaming. Something felt wrong with her hand and now, the memory was coming back to her.

She remembered feeling woozy. She was starting to come around after Nick knocked her out at the front door. The gun and her ex-lover's sinister smile was the first thing she saw when her vision came into focus. Her head felt like it weighed a thousand pounds, as she tried to move it to make sense of her surroundings. She could see a roll a duct tape sitting out and thought it was out of place on the kitchen counter. She couldn't remember how or why she was sitting here.

"Let me see your left hand."

Her mind screamed at her not to listen, but for some reason, her body did as it was told. As opposed to her head, her hand felt weightless. It was drawn to Nick's voice, almost floating to him. Nick took her hand and slid a ring onto her ring finger. Even groggy, Megan could see that it was the engagement ring he wanted to give her the night they broke up.

"This ring was. . . is a symbol of my love for you. You didn't care. You never even put it on. Doesn't it look good on your finger?"

Megan tried to shake her head, but she wasn't sure if her body obeyed. Her head definitely moved in some sort of motion and she felt like passing out again.

Nick smiled. "Our love is forever. This ring is never going to leave this finger."

Nick turned the ring so the diamond was jutting out to the side. He then put her limp hand down on the counter and held it by the wrist. With his other hand, he produced a hammer. "You know what they say...Love hurts."

He brought the hammer down on. The first hit missed and struck her middle finger. Megan cried out in pain. The numbness in her head did not translate to her appendages. The second hit was true. Nick looked at his handy work and hit ring again. Megan fell off her chair into the living room. She raised her hand to her face. She saw her two fingers bent unnaturally and the dented gold band cutting into her ring finger. As she heard the ripping of duct tape, Megan felt herself passing out from the pain.

"What the fuck are you doing!?"

Megan looked up as Nick rushed towards her. Ignoring the pain, she rolled one more time onto her stomach and then, rolled onto her side. With her back to the table, she strained to reach under it. Nick was on her quickly. She tried to kick at him, but he easily picked her up from the floor and threw her onto the couch. He sat next to her and pointed his gun at the front door.

"We're going to sit right here and wait for your girlfriend to walk through that door. I know she has a key. I've watched her come by many of nights and leave in the mornings after you two do what you sickos do."

Megan shifted uncomfortably on the couch, trying to put some space between her and Nick and at the same time, position the sharp end of the nail file against the duct tape. She managed to poke it through the area between her wrists and started to saw.

Megan heard Shannon's car pull up to the house. She heard the car door squeak as it opened, even over the messed-up muffler. For some reason, Shannon left her car running. Perhaps she was having battery issues again. Megan let out a scream, but Nick quickly pushed his forearm against her throat. With his other hand, he pulled out that gun oil rag and began stuffing it into her mouth. She gagged at the taste. At least her nose was uncovered, but the smell still invaded her nostrils.

Nick pointed his gun back at the door. "That wasn't very smart, babe. No wonder you were failing all your other classes. Just sit tight. Once this whore is out of our life, we can begin again."

Megan's eyes watered. The oil was strong and she started to feel lightheaded. I have to hang on, she thought as she regained her grip on the nail file. She started sawing again when she heard the familiar creaks and groans on her porch steps.

Her mind flashed back to the time, Shannon tried to sneak out and sneak back in with groceries to cook her breakfast in bed after their first night together in the house. She failed miserably, but they had a blast cooking together.

"This is so exciting. We're going to be so happy together."

Creak.

And the time Shannon blindfolded her and led her up the steps to a surprise birthday party. Balloons and streamers covered the bare, unpainted walls. Her friends and most importantly, her mother yelled, "Surprise," when she took her blindfold off.

"Nothing will ever get between us again."

Creak.

And the time Megan's grandmother died and Shannon held her, as she walked her up those steps after the funeral. She was there for the good times and the bad.

"You're going to be my little teacher's pet again."

Creak.

Megan blinked her eyes, trying get rid of the tears blurring her vision. In the door's window, she made out the feminine silhouette of her girlfriend. She never knocked. She never rang the doorbell. She always came right in. Megan felt some of the duct tape give away, but she wasn't free yet.

"There's our girl."

Megan kept sawing as the silhouette stood at the window.

"Come on. What is she doing? You don't have to huff and puff. The door is open."

Megan felt more duct tape come loose. She pulled and twisted, but it was not enough. Shannon's blurry form reached up and looked as if she was going to knock. Then, a dark rectangle came into view and was pressed against the window. Shannon turned away and quickly made it down the steps.

Creak. Groan. Creak.

Nick got up and rushed to the door. As he pulled it open and raised his gun, Shannon's beat-up car had already sped out of the semi-circle driveway, leaving a trail of dust. Nick stood there for a second in shock. The sound of the car faded into the distance.

Megan had no idea what was going on, but she knew she still had to get free. Plans had changed. Maybe Nick would go after Shannon.

Nick turned and looked at the outside of the door. He pulled the rectangle off. Megan could now see it was an envelope. Nick pulled up the flap and took out a folded sheet of paper. He stood there reading and after a few moments, started laughing.

Megan's wrists were still bound, but she finally managed to spit out the oily rag. She gasped for clean air. At least, I won't pass out now, she thought.

"You're never going to believe this, sweetheart."

Nick walked over to her and stood in front of the couch with his revolver held at his side and the letter raised in front of him.

"It's time for one of my lectures, my dear. You

always loved them. Well, class is in session." His voiced boomed as if he were in his old classroom auditorium. "Get your notebooks and pencils out. It's time to take notes. Our reading homework for the week was a letter from a lesbian slut named Shannon. Miss Weber, did you do the assigned reading?"

Megan didn't give him the satisfaction of answering. He knew she hadn't read it. He was just playing up the showman in him. It used to make her feel giddy inside when she was in his classroom, but now, it made her sick.

"I'll take that as a 'no'. Miss Weber, if you plan on passing my class, you'll need to do the assigned reading. Now, I'll let you slide this time because you're so damn cute." He smiled and winked at her. "How about I read it to you? It's hilarious.

Meg,

I'm sorry to do this like this, but I can't bear to face you. I think I've made a horrible mistake. My time with you has been great. It really has. It's just that I think I still like guys. They say college is the place for girls to experiment. Well, I think that's all this was for me. I thought this was what I wanted, but I was wrong. Please, don't be mad.

Hopefully still your friend,

Shannon"

Nick put the paper down on the counter, pulled out a red pen, and started making marks on the page. Megan's eyes were watering, despite having gotten rid of the rag. She couldn't believe Shannon was breaking up with her. She didn't even have the guts to face me, she thought. For a few moments, she was alone with her thoughts until she heard Nick laughing once again.

"I hope you can see why I find this so funny. She called you a *mistake.* She wants to be just friends. This all sounds so familiar! It's Shakespearean even! By the way, I also found it funny because of all her spelling and grammatical errors. Seriously, how did you girls get into college?"

Megan quietly sobbed. She no longer cared that her life was in danger. Shannon was her everything. Without her, she thought, I have no reason to go on.

Nick walked over to her, leaned forward, and snapped his fingers. "Hey, Miss Weber. Can you compose yourself for a moment and explain to the rest of your classmates what Shannon was trying to say in this letter? What symbolism can we find in her words?"

Nick pushed the letter towards her. With one

fluid motion, her now free fist swung, driving the nail file through the letter and into the side of Nick's neck. Nick screamed and stumbled backwards. The previously white letter now bloomed red as blood gushed from his neck. He dropped the revolver and it went off. Megan felt the bullet fly by her hair and heard glass shatter as it hit a picture frame on the wall.

Nick fell onto his back. He reached upwards towards Megan and tried to speak, but only gurgles came forth. He managed to grab the nail file and pull it out. Blood sprayed against the carpet. Shannon's note fell to the side. Megan got up from the couch, walked towards Nick, reached across the kitchen counter, and grabbed the almost forgotten hammer. Megan knelt down and grabbed Nick's hand that held the nail file. She brought down the hammer repeatedly, all the while Nick tried to scream. When his hand was a mush of bone and flesh and looked much, much worse than her hand, she picked his gun up off the floor with her good hand and sat on top of Nick. She smiled at him and shoved the barrel against his lips.

"Suck it."

Nick's eyes went wide. His pupils darted in all directions. His good hand slapped against Megan's body, but he was losing his strength fast. She easily pinned it to the floor with her free but crippled hand.

"You like that, don't ya?" she said as she forced his mouth open with the gun. His mouth was an overflowing lake of blood as she dipped the barrel in, like one might do with their big toe to test the water.

"I should have taken European history. I don't know what was worse; having to sit through those boring, two hour lectures, or having to wait two hours for you to get it up and me having to fake it because you could only last a few minutes." She quickly jammed it against the back of his throat. She cocked the hammer back as he gagged, either on the barrel or his own blood.

"Class dismissed."

Megan fired. The gun kicked back, throwing her, some blood, and a couple of Nick's teeth onto the floor. She sat up and looked at the carnage before her. Brain matter and flesh with wet clumps of hair spread out behind Nick's head like gory butterfly wings. She was about to look away when she noticed a square of light appear in his pocket. Then, she heard a buzzing sound. My phone, she thought. She switched the gun to her bad hand, reached into Nick's pocket, and retrieved her phone. The screen told her it was Shannon calling. After a few more buzzes, she decided to answer.

"Hello?"

"Did you get my letter?"

Megan stared down at the bloody paper on the floor. Blood spatter had ruined most of the letter, but she could still see the words, 'mistake' and 'hopefully still your friend'.

"Yeah, I got it."

"I'm sorry. You deserve more than a stupid letter. Can I come over and explain?"

Megan was quiet. She looked down at her dead ex. She turned to the couch to sit down when she saw the bullet hole that went through the picture on the wall. It was a picture of Shannon and her. The bullet hit Shannon dead center on her forehead.

"Meg? Are you there?"

"Yeah, I'm here," she said as she stared at the revolver in her hand. "You can come over now, if you'd like."

"Okay, I'll head back there now. Thanks for understanding, Meg."

"No problem."

Megan hung up and sat down on the couch. All around her was blood and gore. Her house was in shambles. Her life was in shambles.

But she could fix this.

"I can fix this. I can fix us. I can make you love me again. I will make you love me."

Joan began aware of her surroundings. The old man was still sitting next to her. His cane, the one that had the swirling globe on top, was unmoving. She thought maybe she imagined it, but it felt so real. She was so confused.

"My dear, Joan, I have a gift for you. You'll know what do with it when the time is right, but until then, do not open it." Emrys reached into his long black jacket and pulled out an ornate, jeweled box about the size of book.

Placing it in her hands, he said, "Trust me. You'll know."

Emrys got up, while the confused look never let Joan's face. He slowly made his way to the front of the train car. His cane thumped with each step. People noticed him, but he didn't mind. He let them. He grabbed onto the door handle and looked back at Ryan and Marianne. They both were asleep.

Good. It will be easier come later, he thought as he opened the door and headed into the next car.

Shaun Hupp

FATHER

Shaun Hupp

Emrys surveyed his new surroundings, hunting for just the right person. On one side of the car was a group of four black teens. They were all talking loudly, cursing every other word. Across from them was a middle age man and what appeared to be his son. The man kept looking over at the teenagers with a worried look on his face. His son slept.

Emrys could sense what the man was thinking. It filled the air on the car. His biases against the boys of a different race practically bled out onto the floor between them. Emrys's own olive skin tone didn't really match anyone race. He had designed it that way and perhaps if he wasn't so weak, he would lighten his complexion a bit. Regardless, he had his cane.

Emrys moved towards them, each thump of his cane was masked by the rail noises and the teens talking. Something in the man's peripheral vision caught his eye and he looked out the window. It was nothing. When he turned back around, Emrys was sitting next to his son. The man jumped back and opened his mouth to say something. Emrys put one wrinkled finger to his lips.

"Shh. Let's keep the boy asleep. It'll be much easier that way. " Emrys raised his cane so that the man could see the globe atop.

"I understand yourself concern. No. I have no children of my own, but I was one a long, long time ago. You feel threatened. You feel you need to protect your child. There will come a time when that may be true, but sometimes, children will surprise their parents. They can take care of themselves just fine if you let them."

The globe's insides swirled and the man looked on. His son continued to sleep.

"I want to tell you a tale. I'll make sure to keep my voice down. We wouldn't want to wake your child."

THE WORST KIND OF MONSTER

Shaun Hupp

"I'm not lying."

Dustin's mother folded her arms across her chest and gave him one of her patented stare downs. She was in no mood to do this right now. She hadn't showered yet, her hair was a wreck, and she had a lot to do that day. Listening to tall tales from her son was not one of them. Perhaps, she thought, if I had on my mascara, my eyes would look a little more threatening; instead, I probably look like a bag lady. If Frank sees me like this, it'll be an infraction for sure.

"Dustin. . ."

"I'm not lying!"

"Lower you voice, Dustin. Please. You don't want to wake your father."

"Too late," Dustin's father, Frank said as he entered the kitchen. His normally combed, brown hair was sticking up in every direction. He was still in his flannel pajamas. It was clear he hadn't shaved yet by the light stubble around his mouth as it stretched wide for a yawn.

"What's going on, kiddo? Why are you making all that racket?"

"Daddy, there's a monster in the basement and mommy doesn't believe me!"

He sat down at the table where his wife had a plate of eggs and toast for him. He did a double-take when he saw his wife and muttered something about dealing with her later, under his breath. He shook his head and turned back to Dustin. "What makes you think there's a monster in the basement?"

"I heard growling from the laundry chute."

The laundry chute was upstairs, directly outside Dustin's bedroom door. It led directly down to the laundry room that was in the basement.

Dustin's mother was looking into the kitchen window, trying to catch her reflection so she could fix her wild, long blond hair. She knew she'd better eat fast and put on her make-up as soon as possible, or Frank would get upset again. She didn't need any more chores added to her growing list of things-to-do. She hoped her appearance was good enough to be able to eat. She was hungry. The label on a can of peas wasn't facing outward. She had been careless; therefore she couldn't eat the dinner she prepared last night. She sat down at her plate and didn't make eye contact with anyone, as she grabbed her fork. "And I told him that monsters do not exist."

"I'M NOT LYING!"

Dustin's dad slammed his fist down on the table. Everybody and their plates jumped. Dustin grabbed his cup before it fell over, but not before apple juice sloshed onto the sleeve of his favorite camo pajamas. "Enough! Your yelling is giving me a headache and it's disrespectful to your mother. Apologize, right now!"

Dustin pouted and looked down at his untouched plate of food. His blond bowl cut covered his eyes. "I'm sorry, mom."

"Say it like you mean it."

Dustin looked up and his eyes met hers, "I'm sorry, mom." Both of them lowered their faces back towards their plates. His mom's hand trembled as she made an attempt to get some eggs on her fork.

"That's better. Now, son, you're probably just hearing something in the pipes or the house settling. You know how these old houses are. Plus, the water heater is in the laundry room. It's not the first time you've heard something strange."

"I guess. . ."

Dustin's mom reached over, trying to avoid dunking her robe sleeve in his apple juice, and put her hand on top of Dustin's. "You can always crawl into bed with us when-"

Dustin's dad's fist hit the table again. This time, the cup completely tipped over, spilling onto his plate and onto his lap. "Absolutely not! The boy is six years old for Christ's sake. He'd probably be sucking your tit right now if I didn't put a stop to it."

Barely above a whisper, "Language, Frank. . ."

"Well, it's the Goddamn truth. The boy is going to grow up to be a fucking pansy, if you keep babying him. Afraid of monsters? When I was his age, I had already shot my first deer. If he'd go hunting with me, he wouldn't be so scared. A woman, like you, wouldn't understand. When I first held that gun in my hands, I realized how powerful I really was."

Dustin's mom gave her son's hand a little squeeze. "Go to your room and get changed. Then, just play up there for a little bit. Okay, sweetie?"

"Yeah, Dustin, go to your room and play with your little dolls. Pathetic."

As Dustin left his uneaten plate of soggy, ruined food and headed upstairs, he could hear his parents arguing back and forth. He took the stairs two at a time, thanks to a recent growth spurt, and ran for his room.

He shut his door and crawled under the covers of his bed, still wet, but he didn't care. He covered his ears, but could still hear the yelling downstairs. Eventually, he knew the yelling would lead to much more.

If only they believed me, he thought.

*****

Dustin's eyes shot open.

What was that? He thought.

Outside his bedroom door, Dustin could hear the faint growling, that he heard the previous night. He pulled the covers over his head and pushed his pillow around his ears. He was in the same position as earlier except he had on new, dry pajamas. For a few moments, he thought he had silenced the sounds, but they started again. This time the growling was more intense.

I need proof, he thought. They didn't believe me this morning. They always think I make stuff up and then, it makes them fight.

The rest of that day was uneventful. His mom and dad avoided each other, and his dad avoided him. They all sat down together for lunch and dinner, but no one spoke unless it was to ask for something on the other side of the table. His mom packed on the make-up extra heavy today. After dinner, Dustin picked up his toys and hoped he'd get a bedtime story. Disappointedly, he tucked himself into bed and went to sleep.

Dustin threw the covers off. He hesitated for a moment as he put his bare feet on the floor, but then, he realized his monster wasn't under the bed. He searched beneath his bed until he found what he was looking for: his flashlight. He grabbed it and pointed it towards his closed door.

Click.

The beam of light illuminated the plain white door. There was nothing out of the ordinary. So far, so good, he thought. Dustin slowly approached, and his trembling hand grabbed hold of the cold, brass knob. As he turned it, there was a loud snarl. Dustin's hand darted away and he fumbled with the flashlight as he almost dropped it.

This isn't in my imagination. That was real. How can my parents not hear that?

Dustin forced his hand to grab the doorknob again. He slowly turned it, trying to be as quiet as possible.

It's now or never.

He opened the door just enough to poke his flashlight and hand through. The light shined on the laundry chute. It was a white square flap with a white border, that contrasted the hallway's beige tone. There was no sound. No movement. He opened the door and stepped past the threshold. He didn't risk shutting his door. He turned the flashlight towards the stairs to his left. Nothing. He turned it right, towards his parent's room. Nothing.

Dustin walked forward, towards the chute. He pressed the palm of his hand against the flap, lightly enough not to disturb it. He had done this hundreds of times, but now, he felt a kind of terror he had never felt before. Dustin imagined himself pushing the flap open, only to have his hand bitten off by some sharp-toothed creature. Or even worse, a snake-like tentacle could latch onto his arm and drag him down through the chute to the basement, where the monster would, no doubt, eat him whole.

Just do it, he willed himself.

Taking his palm away and using his index finger instead, Dustin pushed the flap open just a little and quickly withdrew his hand. He didn't see or hear anything. The flap swung back into place. Dustin took his flashlight, pushed the flap with it, and held it up. The flashlight showed the wall of the metal duct that went to the basement. He took a deep breath, pointed the flashlight down, listened for any kind of noise, and slowly, inch-by-inch, maneuvered his head through the opening.

His flashlight revealed nothing but a half-full laundry hamper at the bottom of the duct.

Dustin breathed a sigh of relief, and then, a loud growl startled him. He banged his head against the flap trying to get out of the chute and dropped the flashlight. It banged against the sides of the duct as it tumbled down to the basement. It landed inside the hamper.

Dustin whipped his head out of the chute and looked towards his parent's bedroom. He held his breath as he waited for them to burst out of the doorway, wondering about the noise. After a few minutes, he decided they must still be asleep. He was only slightly relieved as he stuck his head back into the chute.

Dustin stared at the flashlight, realizing what it meant. I have to go into the basement, he thought. My mom always does the laundry in the morning and she'll see my flashlight. I can't explain it without saying something about the growling and it will just start another fight.

Dustin had just gotten into trouble early in the week for playing in the laundry chute. One day, he was dropping parachute army men down the shaft. His mother called him for dinner and he forgot to retrieve them. The next morning, she started a load of wash and didn't see the figurines. The strings from their parachutes became entangled in the motor of the washing machine and a repairman had to be called out to fix it. Dustin's father didn't like having to call someone out to fix anything in the house. He considered himself a handyman and if he had to call for help, he took it as a sign of weakness. After three days of working on the washing machine with no success, Dustin's mother called for a repairman, when his father went hunting. He came back early, when his gun jammed, and found the man in the basement. He was furious. The washer got fixed, but that didn't matter. That was another night Dustin spent in his room with his pillow over his head, while things, or people, went bump in the night.

I can't get down there in the dark. I need some light, Dustin thought. Then, an idea came to him. Now, he could also get the proof he needed.

Dustin tiptoed barefoot down the hallway to his

parent's bedroom. The door was open. The moon was shining through their window, casting the shadow of his long and slender frame against the wall. He leaned in and listened. Usually, he could hear his father snoring, but all he could hear was his mother's soft rhythmic breathing. He decided to stay low and out of sight. He got down on the floor and crawled into the room. He could see his mother's silhouette on the left side of the bed. He crawled passed the foot of the bed and noticed that his father's side of the bed was empty.

They were fighting this morning and didn't talk the rest of the day, he thought. He's probably downstairs on the couch again.

Dustin continued to crawl until he got to his parent's long dresser. He slowly stood up, keeping an eye on the bed for movement. There, on top was what he was looking for: His mother's digital camera.

This will get me my proof.

Attached to the top of a camera was a professional flash. Not only did it provide the standard flash when a picture was taken, but it also had a spotlight function. It could cast a steady beam of light. It wasn't as bright as the flashlight, but it would work.

Dustin's mother had complained one day about

being bored. His father didn't want her working; a man provides for his family. He thought since she liked to bird watch, she'd also like to take their pictures. Not knowing anything about cameras, Frank bought the newest, most expensive one, hoping that it would shut her up. She ended up with a camera that she couldn't figure out what half the buttons were for. She barely used it, but she kept the camera out in the open to show Frank how much she loved it.

Dustin grabbed the camera that he had been forbidden to touch, turned to leave, and accidently hit the flash button. A brilliant, bright light filled the room for less than a second. When his eyes adjusted, he could see that his mother was sitting up.

Dustin didn't move. His mother stared ahead at nothing. By the light of the moon, he could see the dark circles around her eyes and her puffy lower lip. It's all my fault, he thought. I caused that fight like all the others. She lowered herself back to the mattress and moments later, he could tell she was sound asleep again.

Taking no chances, Dustin crawled his way back to the door before standing up in the hallway. He clicked on the flash's spotlight function and shined it back towards the stairs, his room, and the laundry chute.

The whole time I was in my parent's room, I didn't

hear anything, he thought. No wonder they don't believe me. The noise doesn't go that far.

Dustin tip-toed back to the laundry chute. He slowly pushed the flap open and looked inside, keeping the camera away from the opening. The flashlight still lay where it fell, casting its light beyond where he could see. He heard no growling.

Maybe the monster is sleeping. I can snap a quick picture and show my parents.

Dustin slowly made his way down the stairs. He was thankful they were carpeted. At the bottom, he got back on his hands and knees and crawled towards the back of the couch. He heard no snoring, but he knew his father had to be on the other side. He made it to the arm of the couch and slowly peered over.

Empty.

I don't understand.

Suddenly, a loud groan came from the basement door. It was usually closed, but now, it was wide open. Dustin knew what was going on.

The monster has my dad, he thought. It's gonna eat him. I gotta save him.

Dustin ran to the basement door and stopped. He

realized that he was only six and any monster that could take his muscular 35-year-old father could easily take him. Still, Dustin decided he had to try. Maybe he could sneak up on the monster and hit him in the head with something.

He crept down the stairs, shining the light at his feet. He didn't want to alert the monster he was coming by seeing the light or falling down the stairs. When he got to the bottom, he clicked off the spotlight and peeked around the corner.

The basement featured one big room with two smaller rooms at the end. The main room was basically a storage area since there was no attic or garage in the house. There were multiple boxes of who-knows-what, an old couch, a television with DVD player that Dustin would watch his father's movies on while he was at work and his mom was busy, and holiday decorations; beyond that, lie the other rooms. There was the laundry room on the left, which also contained the water heater. On the right were Dustin's dad's gun and ammo room. Frank locked his guns up for safety in this room that had a gun vault, and also used it to make his own ammunition.

Since the laundry room didn't have a door, Dustin could see his flashlight as it gave off a little light. He wouldn't need the spotlight on the camera for now. He couldn't hear the growling, so he had no idea where the monster was. He figured he'd look in the laundry room first for the monster and his father and, while there, grab the flashlight. He darted behind a stack of boxes, dropped down to crawl behind an old, stained couch, and stood back up when he got to another stack. He had done this before when the basement was monster free. He liked to come down here and pretend he was a soldier hiding from other enemy soldiers, like in scenes from one of his dad's favorite movies.

He snuck behind a wire shelving unit, packed with boxes, but there was nothing to keep him hidden if he wanted to get to the laundry room. Dustin got on his belly and slowly inched his way to the doorway. Once inside, he grabbed the flashlight and hid behind the dryer. He peered around the corner of the machine and searched the room. Nobody else was in here.

You don't have to do this, he thought. You can just go back upstairs, put the camera back, and go to bed.

But what about dad? Is he in trouble?

At that moment, Dustin heard a thunderous growl. The monster was close by. He didn't see it in here and he didn't see it out there. It had to be in the other room.

Dustin turned the flashlight off and tucked it into the waistband of his pajamas. He couldn't hold both it and the camera, and he needed to take a picture if he was unable to help his dad. At least the police would believe me, he thought. He left the safety of the laundry room and turned to the ammunition room.

How did I not see that before? he thought as he saw the light was on through the large window on the door. His father was insistent on having a locked door, but he didn't like the isolation, hence the huge door window, even if it looked out onto a cluttered basement full of junk. Dustin remembered that his mother begged his dad to put some sort of curtain over the window, when he wasn't in the room. He put one up, but that was an infraction for a woman making demands of a man.

As Dustin approached it, he could see the curtain was tied back. He stopped when he heard a sound that wasn't a growl. It was his father talking.

Thank God, he's okay.

He went to the door, put his hand on the knob, and stopped. He stood at the window and did not understand what he was seeing. His father was wearing his dark blue and stained mechanic's coverall he usually only wore to work. He was walking around and appeared to be fine.

The other man did not.

His father's work table was pushed to the back of the room. In the center of the room, there hung a wiry man in his yellowed underwear from the ceiling rafters by chains around his wrists. His ankles were wrapped together with electrical tape. Pressed against his mouth was a red ball with a leather strap going around his head. Matching the color of the ball, his face wore a crimson mask of blood. The man turned his head towards his father and tried to speak, his voice muffled by the ball gag.

That's the growling I heard. . .

"What's that? I can't hear you," Dustin's father said as he mockingly cupped his ear and leaned towards the man.

The man struggled to speak again, but his dad was already moving away. He grabbed a wrench from the table against the back wall, returned to his captive, and smashed it against the man's ribs. Dustin could hear the bones crack. The man let out a muted squeal and thrashed uncontrollably. The wooden rafters groaned and creaked.

Click.

Dustin's finger accidently hit the shutter button. Luckily, the flash was not turned on. No one noticed. The digital screen showed a preview of the picture. It couldn't compare to what he saw first hand. The blood covering his face was so vividly red in real life. The picture's muted colors did it no justice. His father's war movies never looked this real either.

Dustin looked back up from the camera to see his father picking up a bucket that was in the corner and tossing the contents of it at the man's face. The boiling water hit the man causing suppressed screams and steam to fill the room.

When the air had cleared, Dustin could now see the man's face. He recognized him.

That man is Mister Grady, he thought. No. His name is Grady. Daddy says we don't call those people 'Mister.' He says they are beneath us. He did some handyman work for some people in the neighborhood. He was the one that mommy got to fix the washer and daddy got upset.

"What's the matter? A little hot for you? I thought you people got used to the heat in Africa?"

Daddy says those type of people are dirty and shouldn't be mixing with our kind. They are a different breed. He says they should stick to their own churches and neighborhoods. Anyone that tries to be like one of us should be punished, Dustin recalled.

"Do you want down? Just say 'yes, sir' and I'll let you down."

The man's eyes pleaded with Dustin's father, but no words could escape his gag. He hit him again in the same ribs as before. "I guess you wanted more, you dumb nigger."

Daddy says those people always steal from the local grocery store and the church collection plate. He says they like to get together in groups and attack little white girls and boys.

Dustin's father came back from the table with a pair of garden shears. With a smile on his face, he clamped them on the bottom man's earlobe and cut off a piece of it. Grady screamed as much as he could. "You beasts never listen, anyway."

Daddy always did call them beasts. He says they were beneath dogs, because even a dog could be trained to be useful. Those people couldn't be trained and were a danger to society. They did nothing but hurt good, honest people. This man was a monster, Dustin thought.

Click. He took another picture without realizing what he was doing. The screen showed a close-up of Grady's anguished face. His eyes bulged and his teeth clenched.

His father went back to the table and came back with a metal chain. He wrapped it around his own fingers and started punching Grady in the stomach and face.

Click. The picture showed old and new bruises that could still be seen on Grady's black body.

"I know, I was really surprised to find out that your kind could even afford telephone service. I bet you're wishing you didn't accept my invitation to apologize in person for the way I acted when I found you fixing my washer. I wasn't sorry then and I'm not sorry now."

His father unwrapped the chain and struck Grady with it as if it were a whip. Grady growled in pain.

Click.

Growl.

Click.

Growl.

Click.

His father dropped the bloodied chain on the concrete floor. He unsheathed his knife from his belt and stabbed him in his left thigh. He pulled the blade out and blood spattered against the wall.

Click. The red did not compare to what was sliding down the white wall.

His father went back to the table. When he returned to Grady, he bent down and grabbed Grady's left ankle. His ankles were bound together, but he still tried to kick at him. His dad was strong and blood loss had taken a lot of Grady's strength. When he had Grady's foot firmly pressed against the concrete floor, he took a hammer to each one of his toes.

"This little piggy went to the market. . ."

Smash. Scream. Click.

"This little piggy stayed home. . ."

Smash. Scream. Click.

"This little piggy had roast beef. . ."

Smash. Scream. Click.

"This little piggy should have stayed the fuck away from my family."

Smash. Scream. Click.

"And this little piggy cried wee wee wee all the way back...Hmm. No sense lying to you. You aren't going back home. No one is coming to help you. I hid your pickup truck somewhere people won't look for it. Not that anybody will be looking for you, nigger." With that, His father smashed the rest of Grady's toes all the while, Dustin feverously took pictures.

Standing back up, his father grabbed Grady's face to stop his thrashing. Tears were streaming down his face. Grady stopped moving and his eyes looked over his father's shoulder. They met with Dustin's. There was a silent plead for help from those eyes.

Click.

His father quickly plunged his knife into his eye. Grady went limp. His untouched eye rolled towards the back of his head. Blood flowed from the knife wound down his cheek like tears.

Click.

As Grady's body swayed, his father started to pick up all his tools and put them in a bucket of soapy water. He unzipped his coverall and let it drop to the floor. He stood in his white boxers admiring his work. He started to move towards the door. Dustin thought he was caught, but his father grabbed a video camera and tripod that was by the door, that Dustin couldn't see from his viewpoint. He walked around the hanging body and put the tripod by the gun vault. Dustin watched as his father pulled a DVD from the camera and put it into a case, which then, went into the vault.

Dustin knew he was finished and would come out soon. He quietly, yet quickly, made his way to the back to the stairs. Before he could make it to the first step, the overhead light clicked on and Dustin froze.

He closed his eyes and waited for his father's voice. He heard footsteps and turned around. His father was walking into the laundry room. He threw his coverall into the hamper and turned back to leave. Dustin took off, running back up to the living room, back up the other stairs, and back into his room. He shut the door and climbed into bed. He put his flashlight back under the bed and that's when he realized he still had the digital camera.

He knew he needed to put it back, but he heard footsteps coming up the stairs. He prayed his door would not open. Did he hear me running away? he thought. The footsteps passed by his room and went into the master bedroom. He would have to wait until his father fell asleep to return it.

He was tired, but he needed to stay awake. He decided to go through all the photos he took. He realized, now, that he needed to delete them. He didn't need proof anymore. His father knew about the monster in the basement and his father had taken care of it. There would be no more sounds from the laundry chute, unless his father decided to kill some more monsters.

As he scrolled through the photos, his eyelids felt heavy. He didn't see the blood and gore. He didn't care about Grady. He was nothing. He focused on his father. Dustin had two thoughts that went through his head before he fell asleep.

My daddy is a hero and I need to get into that vault.

Shaun Hupp

The man awoke from his trance. He looked over at his son, who was still asleep. He felt something on his lap. It was a strange, old box. He went to open it, but something made him stop. He knew he had to wait, but he didn't quite know why. Then, he remembered the old man.

He looked to his left and saw the group of teens, still being as loud as ever. Then, he looked straight ahead just in time to see the train's door close shut. He swore the man winked at him just before he vanished.

Shaun Hupp

DAUGHTER

Shaun Hupp

Emrys smiled as he walked through the new subway car. There was so much potential, but he knew he needed more. He looked around. Again, people were glued to their electronic devices. He didn't need a passive sheep. He needed a doer. Then, he saw her.

She was alone, reading an old fashion for these days physical book. Emrys approached her. A smile formed on his aged face. It was some of horror short story book by someone named Andrew Lennon. Surely, this one must have a dark side to her.

Emrys became one with his surrounding once again and waited until everything was just right. Those listening to their iPods had their volume increased, not enough to notice, but enough to mask his movements. Those reading on tablets either sped through what they were reading or slowed down so they everyone reached an interesting spot in their books at the same time.

The old man walked with no one to worry about, not even the young lady he was eying. She was already engrossed in the macabre that she didn't notice him until he sat down front of her.

She gasped and dropped her book on the ground. She watched as the old man slowly reached down and grabbed it. His aching body screamed, but he finally got a hold of it and was able to sit back up.

"Terribly sorry, miss. I didn't mean for you to drop your-" he read the title, "Twisted Shorts. Scary stories thrill you, do they?"

"Yeah," she said, quickly taking the book from his hands. She was obviously freaked out by the stranger sitting across from her.

"I understand the need for reading. It's escapism. And with horror, sometimes the reader has had something so dark happen in their past that they need something even darker to run to."

"Look. I really just want to read my book. I'm not in the mood for-"

Emrys raised his cane. He really thought he would be able to read her before he memorized her, but for some reason, he was drawing a blank. "Tell me. What is the darkness that you flee from?"

Her eyes stared vacantly at the globe.

LAST WORDS

Shaun Hupp

"Wake up."

"Wha. . ."

"Gwen, I need you to wake up."

"Did I oversleep? What time is it?"

"No. I just need you to open your eyes."

"But I'm so tired, baby. Can't you just hit the-"

"Look, bitch. Open your fucking eyes!"

Gwen's eyes shot open at the sound of a voice she did not recognize as her boyfriend's. A stranger's face filled her vision. Frustration showed in his unshaven face, but only for a second. Quick as it had come, his scowl disappeared, and the deep creases in his pale forehead began to relax beneath his shaggy brown hair. Those bright blue eyes remained focused. They seemed to emulate electricity from some unseen force. Gwen couldn't quite place him, but he seemed familiar.

"Where's. . ."

Before she could finish her question, she saw something out of the corner of her eye. Her head snapped to the left revealing her boyfriend, hands and legs each bound together with duct tape in front of him. He was not conscious. It was then that Gwen realized that she too was tied up in the same fashion. She tried to move. Struggling proved pointless; escape seemed doubtful.

Ignoring their captor for the time being, she checked out her surroundings. She remembered something about doing this from a police drama, she would watch every Thursday night when Hank was working. He thought it was silly and morbid, but it might be useful right now. She needed to look past that white, hairy face occupying her field of vision so she could give an accurate description to the police. She could almost hear the words coming out of her favorite actor's mouth, "Watch. Observe. When he is done, you can help bring us back to the scene of the crime so we can get the clues needed to catch him." Gwen just wasn't sure if she and Hank would make it out of this room alive to tell anyone.

How could anybody live here? She thought.

In her groggy state, she could tell she was in a rundown apartment. By the looks of it, it had to be abandoned, but this man could have been living here. Candles covered the countertops and tables, but they were not lit. Light was shining through the cracks in the boards covering the windows. It was daytime. The ceiling consisted of spider webbing, cracks, and peeling paint, that might have been white at one time. There was a portable gas tank in the corner attached to some sort of camping stovetop.

As she tried to commit what she saw to memory, the stranger grabbed her by her long, blonde hair and forced her to face him. It hurt to look at those eyes. I know I've seen him before, she thought. But when? Where?

"While my living arrangements might not win me any awards for interior decorating, you can't beat the neighborhood. You can scream all you want and nobody will hear you."

To prove his point, the man screamed loud and long right in Gwen's face. Spit flew as she flinched away from his gaping mouth and yellowed teeth. His tall and slender frame turned and ran over to the partially boarded window. He screamed out of it and banged on the walls sending dust everywhere.

His lungs finally failed him or the dust got to him. He let out a little cough and smiled. "See?"

Hank groaned. The man's screaming had awakened him. He looked down at his restrained wrists and feet and, then, noticed Gwen trapped in the same manner. He was a strong, muscular guy that went to the gym three times a week, but he wasn't going anywhere.

Looking at their captor's sinister grin, he finally realized what was going on. "Please, mister. Just let her go. You can do whatever you want with me but let her go."

Hank's pleas didn't seem to do anything to help, but Gwen appreciated them. He always had such a giving nature. It was one of the many reasons why she loved him. Despite being ten years older than Gwen and his short, black hair was starting to turn grey, she'd never felt more alive. Having just finished college, and never having had a serious relationship before, she was surprised it had lasted for a year. In fact, just last night was their anniversary dinner. And after dinner, they. . .

"I know you," she realized. "We got in your taxi. But how did you. . ."

"Guilty as charged. Everyone worries about hitchhiking. You never know if the person picking you up is some kind of psycho. Nobody ever questions getting into a taxi. Why not? A stranger is, after all, a stranger.

You guys thought it was such a great idea for a taxi driver to offer bottled water to help sober up customers. It is a great idea. I'll give you that. Of course, you have to be sure you have an honest cab driver that hasn't slipped something into those bottles. In your case, you chose poorly. Had you arrived at that cab twenty minutes earlier, you might have met that honest cab driver. If you'd like to meet him, I have him in the trunk. Don't worry. I'm not charging him a fare."

Gwen and Hank just stared at the man.

"Wow. Tough room. I was kidding, by the way. I knocked the cabbie out with a brick and tossed him in a dumpster. Can you imagine the smell he would have made if I killed him and kept him in that hot trunk? Gross."

"Why are you doing this to us? What did we do to you?" asked Hank.

"You two didn't do anything to me. It's not about me. It's all about you; both of you actually. You see, I've never had a loving couple before. I've tried a priest. I've tried a teacher. I've tried an old woman, who ran marathons, and seemed so full of life. The experience is so different each time, but you two are something extraordinary. I just know it!"

They blankly stared at him.

"Do you two not get it?" he asked. "In layman's terms, I kill them. I take my friendly surgical scalpel, whom you'll meet in just a little bit, and slice them across their bellies to let them bleed out slowly. Don't get the wrong idea; I do not enjoy the killing. I'm not one of those freaks you hear about on the news. What I do is special. I'm not even sure if you two will understand. No one else ever does. It's all about me, me, me. Don't hurt me. Don't kill me. If only they could comprehend what I'm doing here, but they never survive long enough for it to dawn on them. Perhaps this little experiment with two people will make a believer out of one of you; but which one?"

The gangling man crouched down to Gwen's level and got within an inch of her face. His eyes stared as if he were looking through her. She could smell peppermint Schnapps on his breath. He slowly produced the scalpel from his back pocket. It had a red, plastic cap over the top of it with a smiley face crudely drawn in black marker. He pulled his face away and brought the small knife to her eye. He took the cap off and let her see the shiny blade. She could see her own blue eyes, reflected dully in the blade. They paled in comparison to his. "This is my baby," he said. "She has been with me through a lot...to be honest, she's been through a lot of people."

He backed away and Gwen felt slightly relieved. Then, with one quick motion, he slashed Hank's abdomen. After the blade had exited the wound, he shook it, spattering Gwen's face with blood. Her screams of horror were outdone by Hank's screams of agony. Their captor started screaming along with them, moving his head back and forth between them. Then, he began to chuckle as he produced a white handkerchief to wipe the blade clean. After he crumpled the handkerchief into a ball and threw it away carelessly, the man produced a stopwatch from his jean pocket.

Click.

"You see, Gwen. I'm about to become more intimate with your boyfriend than you have ever been. Now before you start thinking, 'but Mr. Killer Sir, I've done this, this, and this, even though I didn't want to, but he did and it was his birthday,' that's not what I mean. Get your mind out of the gutter. Have you ever heard that when you die, your life flashes before your eyes? Well, it's true. I should know since I've had a front row seat to dozens of victims. In those last moments before death, people reveal their lives, their secrets, their most intimate memories. Everyone is different. It's just like going to the movies and walking into a theater at random. Some are sad. Some are happy. Sometimes it can be really humorous. I killed a janitor one time. He lasted five minutes, and all he told me was a Chocolate Chip Cookie recipe his grandmother taught him. I can't call it a total waste because everybody loves my cookies now."

There was silence as Hank grinded his teeth in pain and Gwen couldn't stop staring at the wound. Tears were flowing from her eyes.

"That was a joke. You see, I don't actually bake cookies for anybody. I'm not a frickin' girl scout. I do go door-to-door sometimes, but that's strictly to kill people. Plus, green is not my color."

Hank tried to push his duct taped hands against the wound, but it was pointless. The cut was too deep and Hank's polo shirt didn't offer much protection, neither did the little fat on his stomach. Blood steadily flowed out and began to pool around him. Gwen wanted to move away as it crept towards her thighs but at the same time, she didn't want to leave his side. She tried to cover her legs by pulling her dress lower.

"Okay. Enough with the jokes. I'm not here to entertain you two. According to my handy dandy stopwatch, we don't have much time left now. Hank, my man! You're a dead man sitting. Tell me what you're thinking. The floor is all yours, as it should be because you're bleeding all over it. What do you want to talk about? What's flashing before your eyes? What are your secrets? I'd love to hear from the perfect, loving couple so I can check you off my list. I might even let you kiss her goodbye."

Hank looked up from his wound. He glanced at Gwen and then, back at the psycho. "We're not a perfect, loving couple," he said.

"Oh, please, you think lying to me is going to save you? I was watching you two in that fancy Martini bar. I picked you two out over everybody else because you have that spark every couple longs to have. She's the fucking yin to your yang. Is that the correct usage? I think so because yang rhymes with wang."

Hank shook his head. "No. We're not. I'm a cheater." Tears formed along the bottom edge of his eyelids. "I'm sorry, Gwen. I never meant for you to find out like this."

Gwen sat there stunned. After a few moments to let it sink in, she said, "It's okay, Hank." She had been in short relationships in the past that she ended because of her partners' infidelities. It always turned out to be a one time thing they regretted. In the past, Gwen let her anger get the best of her and she lost many good guys that just made one bad decision. "These things happen sometimes. I am not going to spend the last moments of your life being mad at you. I forgive you."

"You don't understand, Gwen. You're the other woman." Tears streamed down his face.

"No. That- That's not possible. I've been to your apartment."

"It's a friend's apartment who's out of the country a lot. I have a house outside the city. This is why I've always changed the subject when it comes to moving in together. My business doesn't take me out of the city like I told you. It takes me into the city. That's where I met you."

Their captor checked his stopwatch. "You know, it's been five minutes. As revealing as all this has been, my victims almost never last this long. Apparently, I didn't cut you deep enough." He advanced on Hank.

"Please! I'm married," he cried as he pressed himself against the stained, grey wall. He looked at Gwen and then, back at the floor as though he couldn't bear to look at her anymore. As if he could still see her from the corner of his eye, he closed them tight. More tears formed trying to break free. "I have a son. I'm not what you're looking for."

Gwen stared at Hank as if he was a stranger, which wasn't too far from the truth. The tone of his voice and the fact he kept referring only to himself said everything. He is asking for his life to be spared because he is a husband, a father. He was not the man she knew. She was nothing to him.

Hank's revelation did nothing but enrage the man. He kicked Hank in the side of the head. Hank's head hit the wall, knocking off a cloud of dust and plaster. His face, now powdered with dust, turned toward Gwen; forcing their eyes to meet. They were eyes she no longer knew.

"This is just great! Do you know what you've done? This has been a complete waste of time." The man produced a small, black notepad and started flipping through it. "I need to kill a loving couple," he said as he flashed a page at Gwen. She didn't get to see it long, but she saw it long enough to notice many checked off boxes. "I don't need to kill a cheater and his whore."

"I'm not a whore! I didn't know any of this," Gwen shouted at him as if proving herself chaste would allow her to be spared.

"Either way you both are useless to me. You don't understand. The people I kill are good, honest people. When a person dies, there's a lapse between Heaven and this world. As the body's soul leaves, that gateway is open and one day, God will speak to me. He will tell me my true purpose in this life. This connection has to be from someone that is actually going to Heaven. God is not going to speak through either of you. Haven't you guys heard of the Ten Commandments?"

"You're crazy," Hank said.

"Judge not lest ye be judged," the man said as he stabbed Hank with the scalpel. "Are you there, God? It's me, Adam. Nope. I guess I was right."

Gwen cried out again but not as loud or as long as before. This man, Adam, was not so much killing her boyfriend, as he was killing a random person. Still horrifying, but Gwen could now disconnect from the situation somewhat.

With the scalpel still embedded in his stomach, Adam got within an inch of Hank's face. "Let's not make this a total loss. Do you believe in the human soul? You should. It was scientifically proven over a century ago and yet, the world is full of unbelievers. My former employer was one such unbeliever. I was working as a mortician's assistant and one of my duties was to pick up fresh bodies from the hospital. My so-called boss didn't approve of me weighing the deceased at the hospital. There is evidence that the soul weighs twenty one grams. I would race to the hospital, use their scales to weigh the body, and compare notes with weights taken before death. After he had received the third complaint from the hospital administration that I was violating their HIPPA Policy, I had to tell him what I was doing. He called me a fool and fired me. Well, I guess I was being a bit foolish. I should have realized that I needed to be there at the time of death. Perhaps my firing was a blessing in disguise. Now, I get to do what I was born to do. Now, Hank, even though you aren't in my book, your death won't be meaningless. I promise this won't hurt. I want to breathe in your soul."

Hank spat in his face.

In one angry swipe, Adam tore the scalpel through Hank's fleshy stomach. Hank didn't even attempt to stop the blood as it poured out of the wound that stretched across his entire abdomen. He was going into shock.

Adam smiled devilishly until he looked down at his hand. Hank's blood was splattered all over it. Adam gasped, ran across the derelict apartment, and went through a closed door, which proved to be a bathroom. Even though there didn't seem to be any power, Gwen could tell the water worked fine by the hissing sound coming from behind the closed door.

"Gwen. . ."

"What, Han. . ." She stopped. She didn't want to even say his name.

"I'm sorry. I know what I did was wrong. I didn't mean to lead you on. Can. . . Can you still forgive me?"

Gwen said nothing. It would be dead silence if it weren't for the feverish hand washing going on in the bathroom. What is Adam's problem, she thought. Does he have some sort of phobia of blood?

"Please, Gwen. . .I really do love you."

"I loved you," she said and finally turned to meet those eyes. Deep down, she hoped that by saying those words, she would see those loving eyes again. She wanted to see those eyes that she could stare into all night. She needed to see those eyes.

Those eyes were empty. Hank was dead.

Gwen cried. Not so much for Hank, but for herself and the year relationship that was for nothing. She cried for the woman and child she would never meet, for unknowingly enabling Hank to commit adultery. She cried for all those past relationships that didn't work out and for being a fool to think this one would work. At least, she thought, I won't have to grow old alone, because I'll never make it out of here.

"Alright, alright, we've been at this for over ten minutes. You have been by far the-"

Adam dropped the stopwatch and ran over to Hank. After moving his hand in front of those lifeless eyes and lightly shaking Hank's shoulder, Adam slumped onto the dusty floor and lowered his head. "This is all your fault." His voice trembled. "How was I supposed to know that you were a fucking whore?"

Adam leaned in again, within an inch of Gwen's face. "A fucking whore. You don't deserve the intimate touch of my blade. I should slice your fucking throat so you can't talk before you die. I should let you choke on your own blood. God won't speak from those whore lips. No. No. No. Your soul won't be making that connection. You're bound for the lake of fire with the rest of your kind."

Gwen was done. She was tired of being a victim. This wasn't her fault. She needed to fight back. It was her only chance. Before he could react, she smashed her forehead into Adam's nose. This direct hit brought forth a steady stream of blood and a loud squeal from Adam.

"You fucking whore! Look what you've done!"

Adam tried to wipe the blood off his face with his hands, then off his hands onto his pants. He tilted his head backwards, but all this did was allow the blood to flow into his mouth. He threw himself forward and retched.

"No. No. No. No! Get it off me. Why won't it stop!?"

Adam ran into the bathroom, slamming the door behind him. Gwen could hear the water from the sink, but only barely due to Adam's continued curses. That's when she saw the key to her escape.

The scalpel.

He must have dropped it when I hit him, she thought.

Only a foot away from her, Gwen was able to bend forward and grab the gory scalpel. She pulled her blood covered dress up her thighs, placed the knife upwards between her knees, and started sawing at her bound wrists. Adam swore at her from behind the bathroom door. As her hands were now free, she quickly snatched the scalpel and sawed through the duct tape around her ankles. Free at last, she ripped all the tape off, stood up, and set her sights on the door to the apartment. A loud bang brought her attention back to the bathroom door. It was standing wide open.

"Where do you think you're going?" Adam asked in a slightly nasally voice. Toilet paper was stuffed in each nostril.

Gwen extended her arm with the scalpel held high. She started edging forward, towards the door. Adam rushed at her. She sliced left and right, but hit nothing as Adam gingerly stepped back, smiling.

"Just stay back! I'm getting out of here!"

"Oh, please. I kidnaped both you and your 'John' without any problems. I think I can handle myself against an itty bitty woman with an itty bitty knife. In fact, I wonder if you can even-"

Before she knew it, Adam sprang forward and grabbed her wrist that was holding the scalpel. A swift kick caught Gwen in the gut and Adam rammed his shoulder into her face. Gwen tripped and fell backwards. She was horrified to realize that she was back where she started.

Sitting next to Hank.

Adam with the scalpel.

"It's time to end this. I need to get out there and find someone truly worthy of my time."

As Adam advanced, Gwen turned her head away from what was coming. She was looking once more at Hank. She reached out and took his hand. She figured if she were going to die, she would do it with the man she loved. When she squeezed his limp hand, she felt nothing for him. Their love was just a lie. This man was nothing to her. He was not her boyfriend, her soon-to-be husband. He was just dead flesh, bone, and blood.

Blood.

Gwen had nothing left to lose. She reached into the open wound in Hank's stomach. A handful of guts and squishy stuff slipped and slid between her fingers. As she pulled her hand out, the cut expanded around her closed fist and closed against her knuckles. She would never forget that sound. She turned her hand over, and it slowly opened. The amount of guts and gore made her feel queasy, but she had to remember; Hank is gone. Their relationship was fiction. That was the past and she needed to look toward the future. Only one man stood in her way.

Adam's advances stopped when he saw what Gwen had done. His eyes grew wide. He opened his mouth to say something, but Gwen lobbed her gory handful at his head. Adam's face disappeared behind a mask of bloodshed and unidentifiable innards. His legs went out from beneath him as he slipped on the blood and hit the floor. Gwen thrust her hand inside Hank again and pulled out more ammo. Adam turned to run as more gore rained down upon his back. He got hit two more times before he made it to the safety of the bathroom and slammed the door. Gwen continued to throw bloody gobs at the door, crying the whole time.

She looked down at her hands and then, at Hank. She couldn't believe what she had done. A day ago, this man was her world, but he was using her. Now, she was using him. Gwen's tears turned into laughter at the thought. She reached in for more. She found she was less nauseated this time.

"How do you like that, you sick fuck! You want some more blood?"

A wet clump thumped against the door.

"What's wrong, Lady MacBeth? Can't get the spots out?"

Thump.

"Get out here, asshole! I've got a present for you."

Thump.

"Can you guess what it is? It's wet, sticky, and red."

Thump.

"Stop! Just stop! Go. Just leave. Get out of here. You win."

Did he really just let me go, Gwen thought. She had gotten so caught up in the moment that she didn't realize she had a clear shot at the apartment door. She didn't even give Hank another glance as she rushed to the door, but something else stopped her. She heard water running again, except it was different this time.

Is he taking a shower? She thought.

She went to the bathroom door and put her ear to it. Yes, he was definitely taking a shower, this time. Apparently, she did more damage to him than a sink could fix. He could be in there forever especially if he thought she was gone. She had an idea. . .

"Fine. I'm leaving," she screamed out so he could hear over the frantic scrubbing. Instead of going towards to the door, she headed over to the makeshift kitchen and grabbed the portable stovetop. She carried it with its heavy attached gas tank and set it in front of the bathroom door. She cranked the gas on without lighting the burner. Gwen made her way back to the countertop, grabbed a loose match, and stuck the wooden end between her teeth. There was a large sheet of particle board leaning by the window. She lifted it up and placed it firmly against the partially boarded window. Instantly, the apartment was plunged into darkness.

Gwen couldn't rely on her sight. Her hearing wasn't much help either. Thin walls and bad piping made it sound as if Adam's shower could be happening anywhere in the apartment. She didn't want to strike the match just yet. Gwen lost her heels in the skirmish with Adam, barefooted, she tip-toed forward. She was supposed to be gone and didn't want Adam to hear her. Gwen hoped that none of these old boards creaked under her weight. She wasn't a good judge of distance in the dark, but she thought she had to be halfway to the door by now. That was when she slipped and fell backwards. Her head smacked the ancient floorboards. She could feel what was under her. She knew what she slipped on.

Blood.

The shower turned off.

Gwen was still on the floor. She could hear her heart pounding. She figured he heard her fall. Any minute now, Adam would open that door and find her. She shut her eyes tight. Here he comes.

The shower turned back on.

He didn't come out, she thought. He must have heard me fall, then thought nothing of it.

It was then that Gwen realized she had lost her match. She turned over onto her hands and knees and felt around on the floor. Her hands slid through the gory darkness, searching with the sensitive touch of a gifted sculptor. Every time she grabbed something solid, she realized it was some part of Hank, the stranger.

Finally, she knew she had the match between her fingers. She wasn't about to put it in her mouth again.

She figured she might as well crawl to the door now. It would be safer and she was already down on the floor. If she could see, she imagined there would be bloody handprints everywhere. She quickened her pace when she caught the scent of rotting eggs. The gas! She knew she had to hurry. Just when she thought she might have crawled in a circle, her head struck the wall. The thud made her stop and listen to the water pipes.

Please, don't turn off, she thought. Please, keep showering.

The water never stopped flowing, the odd operetta echoing as Gwen continued along the wall searching for the door. When she found the door, she stood up holding onto the frame. Splinters bit into her skin, but she didn't care. She felt around the nearby table until she found what she was looking for. She grabbed a hold of a wax candle with one hand and held the match in the other. She struck the match against the rotting wood of the door.

Nothing. The blood must have coated the match.

She tried again.

Nothing.

The water shut off.

She tried again.

Nothing.

She heard footsteps in the bathroom.

She struck it again.

A flame bloomed and she quickly touched it to the wick of the candle. She knew she was running out of time as the room filled with gas. She slowly opened the door, hoping its creaking would not give her away. She opened it just enough to slip through. When she was on the other side, she quietly, yet firmly, closed the door. She knew she wasn't safe yet, so she ran down the hallway looking for the nearest exit. She shoved open the door leading to a stairwell and took the steps three at a time. She didn't look outside the window before she boarded it up so she had no idea how many stories up she was. The levels all blurred together until the steps ended. She burst through the door and had to cover her eyes from the blinding light.

Outside. I'm outside, she thought. Is it over?

She looked up at the wall of windows. She didn't know which room held her captor and the dead stranger. Just as she gave up on finding the right window, there was a giant explosion. Chunks of brick hurled down on her. Gwen covered her head and ran.

When she thought she was at a safe distance, she looked back to see the fire starting to spread throughout the other windows in the building. Black smoke billowed into the sky.

She looked down at herself and noticed all the blood covering her favorite dress and hands. She could feel the stickiness in her hair and on her face.

Sirens.

What should I do? she thought. That man killed Hank, the stranger, but I'm covered in his blood. My fingerprints were all over that apartment and the murder weapon. Would the fire destroy all that evidence? Would they know who Hank and Adam were? Are they in any criminal database? Hank could be. She realized she pretty much knew nothing about him. Could they go off of dental records? What about Hank's wife and child? If I come forward, will it destroy their family? Is it worse to lose a husband and father to a mysterious fire, or to find out he was cheating and a serial killer murdered him?

The sirens got closer and brought Gwen back to reality. She hastily took off for a side alleyway between two abandoned houses. She found a window that was unlocked and crawled inside. After a quick search of the premises, she found some clothes and shoes she could wear that the former homeowner must have left behind. The water wasn't working, but she found some old two-liters of water someone must have kept in case of an emergency. This seemed like a good time as any to use it.

Inside the smelly, mildewed bathroom, Gwen set down her armful of bottles on the counter, peeled off her clothes, and stepped into the tub/shower combo. She twisted the cap off the first bottle and poured the contents over her. She couldn't find any towels, washcloths, or even a stale bar of soap, so she used some of the clothes she found to wipe the blood away. After emptying three bottles and ruining four t-shirts of a stranger, Gwen finally felt somewhat clean.

Putting on a stranger's old, filthy clothes didn't even faze her. Lying down in the bed of a person she didn't know didn't seem important either. Her old life was just as unknown to her as this place.

I can't go back to my old life, she thought. As soon as the police and firefighters leave, I'll find a way back to my apartment and pack my things. It's time to start over.

Six months later. . .

Gwen had put it off long enough. She finally managed to unpack the last box. She kept putting it off, like maybe if she never unpacked, she'd wake up from this nightmare and her life would be back to normal. Hank would be there. He would ask her to marry him. They would move to a small house outside the city and get started on the family Gwen always wanted. False hope and dashed dreams; the senseless guilt. Hopefully, this move would be the last piece of the puzzle. She had to be away from the memories of Hank. She needed closure.

Now in front of her was an empty white wall and she thought about the life she left behind. After the movers had taken out the last of the boxes from her old place, Gwen was left in her empty apartment with her wall mural. Ever since she lived in that apartment, she had painted something on the wall that meant something to her. Over the last year, she added in several things that had to do with Hank. There was the first rose he gave her. There was the teddy bear he left her after he spent the night. There was the space on the wall that she had been leaving empty, hoping she would one day fill it with a painting of a ring.

She had to paint over it. She didn't care about losing her deposit. If she left it, it would get painted over anyway. She wanted to do it herself. She started off slowly applying the eggshell white but as memories bubbled to the surface, she starting painting faster and sloppier. She had to apply multiple coats as images of candlelit dinners and weekend picnics fought to survive. She shook the roller, spattering her face with white paint. It was done. The mural of her old life was gone.

Now, in her new apartment, she had a blank canvas once again. It yearned for life and it felt good.

Maybe, tonight, I can, finally, sleep without the tv on, she thought.

The television blared so much senseless noise at her all day and night that it became as common as a bird chirping or the wind howling. She needed the noise to drown out the thoughts in her head so she could sleep at night.

She was exhausted and ready for bed, when a news story caught her attention. There was a small fire in an apartment complex. Firefighters quickly put it out and no one was hurt. Despite the differences, the news story made her think back to the day she made it back to her old apartment after the fire.

I'll just change the channel, she thought. No sense dwelling on the past.

When she was within a few feet of the tv, the power went out. Her new apartment was plunged into darkness. The comforting noise from the television had ceased. For a few minutes, Gwen just stood there. She felt as if she was back in that abandoned apartment.

Gwen laughed, "I'm being stupid. It's probably a citywide blackout."

She turned to look out her living room window, only to see the silhouette of a man.

Gwen screamed, turned, and went to run in the direction of the door. She got two steps and slipped. The back of her head hit the wood flooring hard. She turned over and as she pushed herself up, she could feel something on her hands. She knew that texture all too well.

Blood.

That's not possible.

She looked back at the window. It was empty. The man had vanished. There was a clear view of the city. She could see lights on in the building across the street.

She wanted to yell out, "Who are you," but she

thought that might reveal where she was in the apartment. She hoped that if she couldn't see him, he couldn't see her. She also hoped that it was just her imagination playing tricks on her.

She scooted backwards, trying to use the light from the window to see. Her head thumped against something and she realized she couldn't move any further. She reached both her hands behind her and grabbed at what stopped her.

It's just the tv, she thought.

Suddenly, the television turned on. Gwen screamed and jumped away from it. It showed nothing but static and the volume was turned all the way up. She looked around frantically as she thought she heard footsteps, but it was too hard to pinpoint where they were with the tv blasting.

Gwen crawled forward to turn it off when the static disappeared. The news story about the fire returned, except it wasn't about that small apartment complex fire. It was about the abandoned apartment building fire six months ago. The television showed firefighters trying to extinguish the blaze as if it were happening right now.

This can't be happening. How is this possible?

She remembered watching this very news report. She remembered seeing the pile of smoldering bricks. She had wanted to call the police, but she had started the fire that ultimately destroyed that building. She watched in horror, then and now, as firefighters sifted through the rubble. They had found six bodies. Apparently, it was shelter for a few homeless people. She knew she couldn't go to the police. She felt like she was a murderer.

Static.

The television came back on and showed another news report from a few weeks after the fire. Fingerprints were of no use. Dental records were taken of the six people, but only two matches were found. One was known to be homeless when his family was interviewed. The other was Hank. It was verified that he was missing by his family. Gwen broke down, crying uncontrollably when she saw and heard, for the second time, his wife and twelve year old son being interviewed.

Nobody knew why Hank was in the building that day. Police and the family were stumped. The only explanation possible was that Hank was an architect so maybe, he was checking out the building as a possible investment property.

There was no connection to me, she thought. I was scared every time I heard footsteps outside my apartment door. I would silently plead with whoever was out there to leave. No police ever came knocking. Hank had kept me a total secret.

Static.

Gwen couldn't take her eyes off the screen, even though she could hear the footsteps getting closer.

A news anchor said that they had found a gas stovetop and determined that it was the cause of the fire. There were no signs of foul play. The investigators assumed one of the homeless victims had accidently left it on after cooking something. It was not uncommon for homeless people to set up some type of cooking area inside a building, only to have it ignite the already unsafe building. All those deaths were now just accidental.

Static.

Blackness. The television went off.

The lights clicked back on. When Gwen's eyes adjusted, she saw her blood-covered hands. Before she could scream, her head was grabbed from behind and smashed against the television screen. She could feel shards of glass embedded in her face, but only for a moment. She thought the lights were going out again until she realized that her eyelids were closing and there was nothing she could do to stop them.

"Wake up."

Gwen groaned. She had a major headache. Her face hurt.

"Wake up."

No, she thought. I thought I was over this.

"Wake up, Gwen."

It's okay. I can sleep with the tv on a few more weeks and try again.

"Bitch, open your fucking eyes!"

Gwen's eyes opened and she sat up in bed. That wasn't in my head, she thought. Then, it came rushing back at her: the power outage, the television, the man in the window, the blood.

"I let you go and you tried to kill me. Naughty girl. Did you think moving would keep me away? Guess what? I found you."

Gwen couldn't see anything. The room was completely dark, but she could tell by the footsteps and where his voice was that he was pacing around the room. She just couldn't get a fix on him. Gwen quickly slid the drawer open and grabbed her carving knife. The television wasn't the only thing she needed to sleep.

"I've been watching you for awhile now. I was waiting to make my move, but you always had movers in your old apartment. I figured I'd wait and give you a proper housewarming present."

Not being able to tell where Adam was, Gwen felt helpless like she was back in that dirty, abandoned apartment. She didn't have Hank next to her, but she had an idea. . .

"Now, I have you all to myself. I do have to admit, I might look a little different since the last time you saw me."

Gwen took the knife and made a slice down the inside of her thigh. She felt the warm blood flow down her leg. She pushed her hand down onto the wound and flicked blood out into the darkness hoping to hit Adam.

"Thinking back, it's quite funny. This whole time I was waiting for God to answer me. Turns out, someone else did."

She flung more and more blood in every direction. Suddenly, those footsteps stopped. Then, there was laughter.

"That's not going to work, Gwen. I should thank you. You see, my phobia of blood touching my skin was really holding me back. Now. . ."

The lights flipped on. Standing across the room by the switch was something that was beyond any nightmares she had ever had. What stood before her could barely be described as a person. It wore no clothes. Brown and black burns covered its entire body. It was hairless with flaky, cracked skin.

As it struggled to walk towards her, she could see bones poking out and its muscles moving as if there was nothing covering them. Burnt scabs cracked as it walked, blood and pus filling the gaps. She screamed at her body to move, but it wouldn't listen. The knife in her hand fell from her useless hand and clattered onto the floor. This corpse-like thing crawled into bed with her and showed her a blackened scalpel it had hidden in its palm. Its fingers were nothing but blackened bones.

"Now, I have no skin to worry about."

Gwen screamed as Adam stabbed her in the stomach repeatedly with the scalpel. Blood flew from her gut and splattered all over him. During his frenzy, he even opened his mouth, trying to catch some of it. When he was pleased with what he had done, he sat up and stared at the small knife with a look of glee. Then, he licked the blood off the burnt knife and crawled back on top of Gwen. As her life was quickly fading, the last thing she saw was Adam's hideous burned face inches from hers. He no longer had any skin around his mouth or lips covering his black teeth to stop the saliva from dripping onto her. His nose and ears were gaping holes where the blackness inside seemed to go on forever. But it wasn't the face that got to her, it was those unmistakable eyes; those bright blue eyes full of madness, but they had changed. Now, his eyelids were completely gone. His stare was unblinking. His eyes dried out and red. She shut her own eyes, trying in a feeble attempt to wish him away. She could sense him lower his mouth next to her ear. She could smell peppermint and sulfur.

"You'll have to speak up, girlie. I'm a little hard of hearing now." Gwen could feel the coarse, burnt flesh press up against her cheek as Adam put his ear hole next to her mouth.

"Any last words?"

The End?

Or a new beginning?

"This better be good."

Detective Sergeant Thomas Turner had worked the last three weeks straight. The bags under his eyes showed it. If he had a wife, she'd be pretty angry. Still, being called into work on his day off was beyond infuriating. Can't one of the other detectives handle this? he thought. I need my beauty sleep.

Tom snorted at the thought. Me? A beauty? There's a joke.

"We just figured you'd need to see this," Detective Andrew Sanford said, nervously. "It's big."

Detective Sanford was the new hotshot in the department. He was young, in good shape, and still had all his hair, all things Tom couldn't say about himself. Despite that, Sanford had an irritating habit. He thought every little thing had the potential to be a major breakthrough in a case. One time, he was determined to have every fingerprint lifted off a gas pump to catch a suspect. Nobody had the heart to tell him that those nozzles have had about the same number of hands on them as Tom's ex-wife. That, and it had rained that morning.

Sanford led Turner through to the back of the station and into the police garage. Sitting inside, surrounded by other detectives and forensic technicians, was a taxi cab. Something looked a little off about it. It looked like it was covered by a thin layer of black soot.

"So, what's the story here, Sanford?"

"A while back, a cab driver reported that he was assaulted and carjacked. Well, we finally found it."

"I fail to see why I need to be here," Tom said, annoyed.

"It was near the old Mitchum Apartment building that burned down."

"So? Lots of scumbags dump stolen things off in that area when they get bored. No prying eyes. Get to the point, Sanford."

"Well, to help identify the perp that attacked that cabbie, we had the taxi dusted for prints. What we found was quite shocking."

Tom noticed that all the other detectives and the technicians had turned and were watching the two of them. Some looked excited. Others wore worried expressions. What the hell is going on? He thought.

"There were four different sets of prints,"

continued Sanford. "Naturally, the cabbie's were in there. After him, things get weird. We found the prints of one, Hank Mathews."

Thomas felt his jaw slightly drop. "The same Hank Mathews that died in the Mitchum fire?"

Sanford nodded. "The second set of prints belongs to a Gwen Baker."

Thomas made an effort to keep his mouth closed. "As in the Gwen Baker we found the other day massacred in her apartment?"

Sanford nodded again. "Yes. They matched the prints we took off her body. All of their fingerprints were found in the backseat of the cab. As far as we know, they had no connection to each other. We're going to have to look into how or if they knew each other."

"And the fourth set?" asked Thomas.

"They belong to a man named Adam Booth. We couldn't find out much about him. He has no current address so he might be a vagrant. His prints were found throughout the cab. We pulled up an old picture of him from a prior DUI arrest and showed it to the cabdriver. He verified that Adam stole his taxi."

Before Tom could speak, the head of forensics, a

weasel;y little man in thick, black glasses, came up to them. He couldn't remember his name. He didn't really care.

"We have the results back from the half-empty water bottle that was recovered. There were traces of Flunitrazepam inside. We also found three sets of fingerprints on the bottle: Hank's, Gwen's, and Adam's. DNA evidence confirmed that only Hank and Gwen drank from the bottle."

Sanford nodded to the tech and motioned to leave them alone. "Looks like this Adam stole the cab, drugged those two, and took them back to the apartment building. Gwen and Adam must have escaped the inferno. Perhaps she got away from him and he, just now, found her and killed her."

Tom had a bad feeling about this. Something wasn't quite right. Sanford's theory fit and somehow, it didn't. He wished he could just go home and take the rest of his day off. He knew he couldn't. Sanford really did find his big breakthrough and they had to act on it.

"We need to find Adam."

To be continued. . .

Shaun Hupp

The woman's eyes unfocused from cane. She looked up at Emrys with tears in her eyes. Emrys knew they were mostly likely from realizing she had dredged up old memories she had tried to bury. Those tears streamed down her face and fell across the cover of her book. Before she could speak, Emrys handed her the same box he had given the other two passengers.

"Don't cry now, young reader. You're about to be part of something wondrous shortly. I'm sure your pretty face will be all over the news. Perhaps your mother will even see it."

She was quiet. Emrys had done what he needed to do so he stood up and made his way to the door. As he passed by her, she reached out and grabbed him by the sleeve.

"What happened to Adam? Did they stop him?"

Emrys smiled. She was a true reader, always wanting to know what happened next, reading on through the night. "That, my dear, is a tale for another time. But trust me... It's not going to end well for anyone in that story."

She let go and went back to reading her book. The wooden box on the seat next to her.

Shaun Hupp

SON

Shaun Hupp

Emrys was worried. The next of couple of train cars he entered were empty. He didn't have all that he needed yet. There had to be one more person riding the rails this late at night. His knees buckled several times and he was forced to use the seats along with his cane to walk.

Finally, he went through a door and found himself in another car full of teenagers. His eyesight had blurred. He tried to focus on who was there. There was a group of four in front of him: two boys and two girls. Several rows in front of them was a lone boy. The group was taunting and throwing things at the back of his head. The boy just sat there.

He's the one.

Emrys tried to take control of the environment, but he was too weak. He stumbled forward, getting hit by flying pieces of food. The boy didn't acknowledge him when he sat down in front of him. Much like the last girl, he was trying to escape reality.

The boy was obese, taking up two of the small subway seats. Clearly, this was the reason the others were making fun of him. Emrys thought it was quite sad. People are different. If these kids gave him a chance, perhaps they would enjoy each other's company. This boy just needed a chance to shine. Emrys would give him that.

"Don't let them get you down, son. They don't realize just how special you are."

Again, he didn't even acknowledge the man in front of him. An M & M bounced off the back of his head.

"Please, tell me your name. I want to officially meet the person that's going to save my life."

He looked up at Emrys. "Save your life?"

"Yes. I have faith in you, but you need to have faith in yourself," Emrys said before a fit of coughing. He pulled his hand away and saw blood on his palm.

I'm running out of time.

"My name is Luke. I don't understand how I can save your life. It looks like you need a doctor."

Emrys smiled and brought up his cane, almost dropping it. His fingers didn't seem to listen to what he wanted them to do. Regardless, the globe did its thing and Luke was hooked.

"I don't need a doctor, Young Luke. There's no hospital in the world that could help me. But you, you can help me. You just need to listen to my story. Hopefully, I can finish it."

POUND

Shaun Hupp

Chapter One

"Honey? Hell-ooooo? Terry, are you home?" Trish called out before walking into her house. She listened. When she heard nothing but silence and birds chirping, she looked over her shoulder at Grant. "Coast is clear, lover boy."

Grant closed the door behind him and within seconds, Trish was on him, their bodies and mouths intertwined. Flesh and fabric fought in a war of friction as hands blindly groped and grabbed at anything gratifying. They crashed onto the leather couch, Trish on top. Grant's hands held firmly onto her ass, pressing the swell of his crotch against her. His erection strained against his slacks and had been ever since they left the office. He reached down, trying to free it, but Trish knocked his hand away and sat up, straddling him, showing him who was in charge.

"Not so fast," she said, slyly. "My husband has a very important meeting out of town and he said he was going to be home very late tomorrow. We've got plenty of time. Let's slow down and enjoy it."

She got off him. He went to stand up as well, but she playfully pushed him back down. "You stay here. I'm going to get us some champagne to celebrate a long day of work and what will be a long night of play."

As she walked away, she unbuttoned her silk blouse and threw it back at him. Then, she slowly unzipped the back of her black skirt and let it drop to her ankles. She let him admire the back of her perfectly toned and tanned body. She had purchased this outfit just for him: black nylon stockings, attached to a lace garter belt with matching bra and thong, that complimented her dark, curly hair. She smiled seductively over her shoulder and closed the door to the kitchen.

Trish went over to her mini champagne fridge and pulled out a bottle she knew Terry wouldn't miss. Then, she decided *fuck it* and grabbed one of his favorites.

Maybe if you were home once and a while, you'd get to see me in one of these outfits that goes on your credit card, she thought as a single tear formed at the corner of her eye. *And maybe if you didn't work so much, I wouldn't be on boyfriend number five.*

She quickly wiped the tear away, checked her mascara on the side of the toaster, and grabbed two champagne flutes from the cabinet. *Doesn't he realize how lonely I get?* she thought. *Would he even care if he found out about all these flings?*

Trish filled up the two glasses and headed back. She pushed those hurt feelings deep down and prepared herself a night that would hopefully make her feel wanted again, even if it were just meaningless sex. To Grant, she was just a hole that he planned on filling. Oddly enough, she felt likewise.

Shaun Hupp

Chapter Two

"Do you want to fuck me?"

"Hell yeah."

"I've been so lonely and so, so horny. I need a big, strong man that can satisfy me. Can you satisfy me, baby?"

"You know I can."

"Do you want to put it in my tight. . ."

"Yes."

". . .wet. . ."

"Yes."

". . .Pu-" A pop-up appeared on the screen with a flashing button that had the words: Click here to view the full video on our website.

"DAMN IT!" I screamed and hit Esc on the keyboard to exit full-screen mode. There were millions of free porn videos online. I wasn't about to go to a pay website and give them my credit card information. That's how I got my card taken away by my parents last time and I didn't need that happening again. I needed it for gas or it was back to taking the bus to school. Not that my old beater car was any less embarrassing.

I grabbed my jumbo-sized, fast food cup and took a drink. And without gas for my POS car, I would be stuck eating the food in the house. My mom couldn't cook to save her life. No wonder both my parents were rail-thin. I reached over to the yellow paper-covered brick and unwrapped my triple bacon, double cheeseburger deluxe with extra mayo, extra barbecue sauce. I held that wet sesame seed bun with both chubby hands, forced my mouth as wide as it could go, and took a big bite. It was orgasmic.

"Enjoying your burger, fatty?"

I put my food back down on the greasy paper and spun around in my computer chair. There, leaning against my closed door, was Tony Miller dressed in his standard, custom-faded and torn jeans and designer T-shirt touting whatever teen clothing store was the popular trend these days. His perfectly trimmed short, blond hair made my hair look like my mom cut mine. . . which she did.

"I *said,* 'Are you enjoying your burger, fatty'?"

I rotated my chair back to the computer. *Don't pay attention to him; he'll leave you alone,* I thought. I took another sip from my sugary drink.

"Keep telling yourself that, you fat fuck! Fat Matt,

Fat Matt had a heart attack. Fell over and killed the cat. Woke up and had a flat snack!"

My drink trembled in my hand; ice cubes knocked against one another. I took enough abuse from him and his friends all day at school and I wasn't going to do it at home too. "SHUT UP!" I whirled around and flung the drink at him. . . only to see it explode against the door. Brown liquid ran down it and pooled onto the carpet.

I was alone.

"You're not real," I whimpered. "You're not real."

Back to the computer screen, I turned. *I'll clean up that mess later or I'll just leave it. It's not like anyone will care,* I thought. My carpet was already covered in stains anyway. I was just glad my parents weren't home to hear me. It was Saturday; my mother wanted to go to the mall as usual and wanted me and my dad to go with her. I pretended to be sick, which isn't too hard when you sweat all the time. I just couldn't risk my mother dragging me into the Big and Tall store for new pants and Tony (the real one) and his friends seeing me. They didn't need any more ammo than they already had against me.

I quickly found another video that looked like it would do. I clicked the picture of the blond, teenage girl and waited for the video to load.

"You know. . . If that girl went to our high school, she wouldn't even look at you, but give me a couple of days and I'd be balls deep in her."

Ignore him.

The video loaded pretty quickly despite the crappy internet connection due to my house being out in the boonies. The girl with the bad dye job looked seductively into the camera. She was wearing a red string bikini, but it quickly disappeared in the next scene. This video was yet another where if you wanted the whole video, you had to pay. Nevertheless, I hoped it showed me what I needed to get off.

The girl's breasts were almost non-existent. Usually, I liked them 'bigger the better', but I wasn't too picky right now. An off-camera hand came on the screen and pinched one of her brown nipples. She moaned. A deep male voice said, "Are you ready to suck this cock?"

A laugh. I looked over at my bed where Tony was laying down, tossing and catching a baseball. "I bet she couldn't even find your dick under all that fat."

I ignored him, increased the sound on my speakers, and looked back to the screen. Already the girl had the cameraman's penis in her mouth. *This is what I needed.* I quickly stood up, pulled my grey sweatpants down, and freed my own penis from my boxers. I stroked it as I watch her slide her mouth back and forth. From this point of view, I could pretend his dick was my dick.

The man moaned. I moaned. Tony laughed. "Your wang is so small and your hand is so fat, I can't even see what you're doing over there."

Ignore him.

I turned the volume up again. The scene cut to the cameraman giving it to her from behind doggy-style. He said,"You're so fucking wet." My hand felt dry. I reached over, rubbed my hand on the greasy burger wrapper, and went back to jacking off.

"Oh, that's so fucking gross. You are seriously messed up, Fatty Matty."

"SHUT UP!" I started beating faster and closed my eyes, listening to the girl screaming with pleasure. My greasy hand felt good against my shaft.

"Why don't you put some ketchup and mustard on it too while you're at it? Maybe, you could-"

"SHUT UP!" I hurried over to the empty bed and pounded my fists against the mattress over and over.

Left, right, left, right. I shut my eyes and let the rage inside of me take over. Left, right, left, right. Soon, I didn't even feel like I was in control of my body. Left, right, left, right. When I was finally out of breath, I opened my eyes and stared down at the oily hand stains on my bedspread. Yet another mess no one would care about. I stood up and caught my reflection in the hanging wall mirror. My easily 300lb frame barely fit within its edges. Sweat had plastered my brown hair to my forehead. I had my pants around my ankles, my limp penis barely hung outside my grease stained boxers, and tears streaming down my face, as orgasmic screams filled my bedroom.

I pulled my sweatpants up, walked back over to the computer, and exited out of the internet. Screams of ecstasy that echoed off the walls turned to silence except for my heavy breathing. I was done. It just wasn't happening for me. Tony had gotten to me once again.

The front doorbell rang.

I jumped as much as my fat frame would allow. My parents rarely got visitors and I had no friends. It could be a salesman or maybe a neighbor.

It could be Tony.

It's not Tony. Tony doesn't know where I live, and

if he did, he certainly wouldn't ring the doorbell and risk getting my parents.

I walked over to the window and peeked through the blinds. I couldn't see the front door, but I could see the driveway; it was empty. It had to be someone from one of the homes nearby, but even nearby was quite the distance.

The doorbell chimed again. With my parents away, I could ignore it. Any neighbor would just think that the whole family was out. We didn't have a garage so whoever it was could see the family car was not home. My car was, but a neighbor could assume we took one car for that 'perfect family' outing.

I chuckled at that thought.

Now, there was a banging on the door. *Jesus*, I thought. *Maybe it was some sort of emergency.* The closest neighbors to us are an elderly couple. Perhaps something was wrong.

I opened the door to my room, stepped over the puddle of cola, and headed downstairs. Each wooden step groaned as my foot hit it. I tried to tell myself that it was an old house, but my parents never had such issue.

I reached the door. *Still time to change my mind. No. What if something happened to Mr. Myers? He has a bad heart. I would feel awful if I could have helped.* I grabbed a hold of the doorknob and opened the door.

It wasn't Mrs. Myer or even Mr. Myer. My hand trembled on the knob as I gave witness to only what could be described as an angel fell to Earth. Had I checked the peephole, perhaps being given a tiny glimpse would have prepared me for taking in her beauty entirely. Her impossibly long legs gave way to jean shorts that were way too short to be school appropriate. But she was no girl. She was a woman in her mid-twenties. Her long, brown hair almost matched the shade of her tanned skin. She gave me a perfect smile.

"Hi. Sorry to disturb you like this. Umm. . . My car broke down a little ways down the road and this was the first house I came to. Do you mind if I use your phone? You know. . . to call a tow truck."

I tried to get my mouth to move, but it wouldn't respond. This had happened to me before at school, and this was where the girl usually called me a perv and told me to stop staring at her. This woman wasn't like that. She gave me a little smile and put her hand on my shoulder. "I'd really appreciate it. Yours is the first place I've seen in a while. I'd hate to keep walking. My feet are killing me."

Still unable to talk, I just moved my bulky body aside and let her in. Her high heeled sandals clacked on the tile of our entryway. She turned around and flashed that smile again. "Nice place you got here. I'm Nikki, by the way."

"My parents'," I blurt out, finding my voice.

"Excuse me?"

"It's my parents'. I mean, I live here, but they own it. I'm going to get my own place real soon after I graduate. . . Not that I'm some young kid. I'm eighteen for sure. MATT! My name's Matt."

I silently kicked myself for being so awkward. *Now, she thinks I'm some kid,* I thought. *I should have told her this was my house and I was an available bachelor.*

She gave me an odd look. "Uh, huh. The phone. . .?" She crossed her arms and pointed to the right, which was the living room and to the left, which was the kitchen. I felt the stirring in my crotch as I watched her arms push her breasts up and together. I quickly grabbed a random book my mother left on the front table and used it to cover up my growing erection beneath my sweat pants.

"Sorry. It's in the kitchen," pointing to my left,

her right.

She turned and walked through the open doorway. I followed behind her. I was about to show her on the wall by the fridge where the phone was, but she found it on her own. She grabbed it off its cradle and started dialling. She looked back at me. "Thanks again. I really appreciate this. So do my feet."

I nodded, still hiding my erection. I tried to think of other things: baseball, 9/11, my mother hula dancing. It wasn't helping. It was hard not to look at those curves on her. A bead of sweat formed on her forehead, slid down to her neck, and finally disappeared into the chasm of her breasts.

"Woah. Check out that sweet piece of ass!"

Boner gone, I put the book on the counter and looked at Tony across the kitchen's island. He was eating an apple obnoxiously loud for someone imaginary. "Seriously, Fatty Matty. I didn't think a girl would ever come into your house unless it were against her freewill. I wouldn't worry about covering your boner either. What is that thing, like two inches?"

Angrily, I looked away to ignore him and realized Nikki was talking to me. "-your address? I need to tell the tow truck where to come."

Tony laughed. "You can tell me where to cum anytime."

Ignoring the voice, I gave her my address, which she repeated into the phone. It was quiet while she waited for a response. I could hear soft hold music. The crunch of an apple almost made me jump. I looked over at Tony. He put down his apple, held up the 'okay' sign with his left hand, and slid his right index finger in and out of the circle.

"Okay. Okay. I'll be waiting," Nikki said into the phone before hanging it up. "I've got good news and I've got bad news. The good news: A tow truck is coming. The bad news: They said it would take a couple of hours. Apparently, they've had a really busy weekend and since this is pretty much in the middle of nowhere; they can't justify dropping everything. I know... I'm probably inconveniencing you."

Tony laughed. "Yeah. You're cutting into his jacking off time."

"No. No. No. It's no inconvenience, really. I was actually kind of lonely with my parents gone and all. I could use the company."

That perfect smile. "Well, I'm glad I could help then." She let out a playful laugh that was divine. "If I could just ask for one more tinsy, tiny favor: Can I have a glass of water? It was a long, hot walk."

"Of course." I grabbed a glass out of a cabinet and went to the sink. My parents had installed some super-fancy water filtration system that attached to the end of the faucet. Unfortunately, I never learned how to use it since I didn't drink anything that wasn't caffeinated and carbonated. After randomly hitting a few buttons, I think I got it working and filled up a glass.

"That's right," Tony whispered in my ear. "We don't want that mouth of hers to get too dry for what you have planned later."

"Shut up," I muttered.

"What was that?" Nikki asked.

"Nothing. Nothing," I covered. "I just said that the faucet was stuck a little, but I got it fixed." I handed her the glass, which she quickly put to her mouth and sucked down.

"So. . . You like that book?" she asked, setting the glass on the counter.

I didn't realize what she was talking about until I followed her eyes to the book on the countertop that I had been using to cover my erection: 50 Shades of Grey.

My eyes went wide. "No. No. That's my mom's book. I. . . I just realized she left it sitting out and I thought I'd put it away for her."

"That's nice of you. I read it a while ago. It's a pretty steamy book. I don't think I'd leave it sitting out like that. I have my copy tucked in my panty drawer."

Panty. Drawer.

I must have turned bright red because Nikki quickly said, "Let's change the subject, okay? Ummm. . . How about you give me a tour of your house? I mean, if you think that would be okay with your parents."

Tony was at my ear again. "Give her the tour, Matt. Show her your bedroom. Show her your panty drawer." He burst out laughing.

Asshole.

"My parents won't mind. They won't even know you're here. They shouldn't be home for hours."

There's that smile again.

Shaun Hupp

<u>Chapter Three</u>

Trish set the two glasses down on a table outside the kitchen door. She was not happy. She was hoping for a little drinking, a little foreplay, and then, the main event. What she saw, his clothes thrown all over the floor and his bare feet up on the leather sofa's arm, was not what she had in mind. If the past was any indication, he probably got started without her.

"Grant, I told you to wait," she said as she walked over to him. "Don't you ever listen to me or do you only listen to your-"

She stopped dead in her tracks. Grant's naked body was still, his eyes glazed over, blood flowed from a large indent in his forehead and puddled on the cushion. She screamed, turned around to run back to the kitchen, but was halted again.

A very tall, muscular man Trish had never seen before stood at the kitchen door. His matching camo jacket and pants seemed so out of place in her elegant home. He picked up one of the flutes and took a sip of champagne. He lowered the glass and licked his lips, but Trish was too busy staring up at the deep scar running up his bald head to notice. "Mmmmm. Sometimes I do like to kick back and appreciate the finer things in life." He set the flute down on the table and picked up a crude, handheld sledgehammer that had not been there before. Trish could see blood and bone fragments on the flat end. He pointed it at her, sending a few blood drops her way that struck her face. "Interesting. Now is usually when they start running."

And she did. She rounded the couch, headed for the library to get away from the man and the gory scene in the middle of her living room. She heard heavy footsteps not too far behind her.

<u>Chapter Four</u>

God! The shit I have to put up with, I thought as the fat kid led me into the living room. I quickly looked around: old tv, empty mantle, bare walls. *NOTHING OF FUCKING VALUE!*

"Well, this is the living room."

No shit, Sherlock.

"This is the room where my parents and I watch tv."

This is the room where I'm going to hang myself if this turns out to be a bust. Months of planning and watching down the drain, I thought. *This brat wasn't even supposed to be here. He always leaves with his parents. At least, I'm glad I had knocked on the door before I attempted to break in.*

"Over here is the downstairs bathroom-"

That I bet you clogged many of times.

"Well, that's pretty much it."

I can't believe I'm going to say this. . . "What about upstairs?"

He was quiet for a moment. "There's just the bedrooms and another bathroom."

Here we go. "Well, okay. Let's continue with the tour."

"You. . . You want to see my bedroom?"

"Sure. We still have an hour or so to kill."

Chapter Five

Trish put Terry's giant oak desk between herself and her attacker. She reached behind her, grabbed an armful of books, and started throwing them at him. The man laughed and knocked some of them out of the air with his hammer.

"Swing batter batter, swing!" he yelled as he sent a book flying back at her. She easily avoided it, grabbed an oriental vase, and chucked it at him. He tossed the hammer on the table and caught the antique with both hands.

"Fuck, girl!" He carefully set it on the desk and picked his hammer back up. "Those things are pricey. I don't think your husband would appreciate you destroying the house. . . or fucking your co-worker. Shameful is what it is."

Before Trish could grab something else to throw, the giant of a man leaped on top of the table and swung his hammer at her face. She dodged but fell backward, hitting her head on the wood floor. She was dazed for a moment, but that was all it took as the man's boot came down on her hair. She tried to pull away and felt her curls being pulled from her scalp. His other boot came down on the other side of her head. She was trapped.

"Tisk, tisk. That was too easy. I was expecting a challenge. I like to have fun."

Trish started to cry. She thought about punching him in the crotch, but her short arms couldn't compete with his long legs. Then, she thought maybe she could go for his crotch a different way. With one final sniffle, she said, "I like to have fun too. Maybe we could have fun together."

The man looked confused at first and then, gave her a sinister smile. He stepped back freeing her, but still held onto his bloody hammer. "What did you have in mind, little lady?"

Trish sat up and tried to mentally prepare herself for what she was going to do. *Just pretend he's a new co-worker that just started in the office,* she thought as she unhooked her bra and let it drop. He didn't seem impressed so she seductively crawled over to him. No reaction until she slid her hand slowly up his pant leg. By what she felt, he definitely liked what she saw.

She started to unzip the front of pants. "I usually like to know a man's name before I do something like this."

He was silent and, after a moment, said, "Devin."

Trish wasn't sure if he was hesitant about

revealing his name or he was making one up on the spot. Logically, he would have picked something like 'John' and not 'Devin'. "Okay, Devin," she said as she reached into his fly. "Let's have some fun."

Shaun Hupp

Chapter Six

"Why do you want to see my parents' room?"

"We've got hours. Do you have anything else in mind we could do?" Nikki gave me a smile that made me melt.

Tony had spent the last couple minutes walking behind her and dry humping the air like he was doing it doggie style. "Here's your chance, Fatty Matty. Go for it!"

"I guess we could look around a bit."

"Puuuuuusssssssssy," Tony shouted in my ear. It was hard to ignore him, but I did and I opened the bedroom door.

I had seen my parents' bedroom before and I knew it wasn't really tour-worthy. I probably hadn't been in there for at least a year, but it never changed. Just like the rest of the house, my parents didn't believe in throwing their money around and living the lavish lifestyle. It contained a queen-sized bed, two dressers, a television, and painting my parents got twenty-five years ago as a wedding gift.

"Well," Nikki said. "This room certainly goes with the rest of the house, I guess."

"I'm sorry. I told you it was nothing special."

She walked around a bit, and Tony and I got an excellent view of her ass hanging out of her short shorts. "Damn, Matt. If you don't hit that soon, it just proves that you're ga-"

Tony was quiet, but he was still staring at her ass. It was as if he noticed something, which meant on some level, I noticed something. Then, I saw it. In the back pocket of those tight shorts, was the outline of a cell phone.

If she had a cell phone, why did she need to use my phone? I thought. *I guess it was possible that she couldn't get cell reception out here. Half the time, my parents had problems and just used the house phone. But why hadn't she mentioned it?*

She walked over to the painting that was hanging on the wall next to the closet. It was a reproduction of the Norman Rockwell painting where a young couple was signing their marriage license. She seemed fascinated with it and then, she quickly turned back to me.

"Did you hear that?"

"Hear what?" I asked.

"I thought I heard a car door."

It was too soon for the tow truck, I thought. *Oh, no. My parents!*

Chapter Seven

I put my hand over my mouth because I almost started laughing when the fat kid waddled over to the window. *Control yourself, girl. Remember the mission.*

With his back to me, I grabbed the edge of the painting and pulled it slightly away from the wall.

Jackpot! There was a wall safe behind it. I knew there had to be something worthwhile in this house. It would be so much easier to load up my car with cash than it would valuable antiques like I thought I was going to find here.

I had done my research on fat boy's daddy. The guy owned multiple factories all over the state. When I was able to pin down his address, I knew this would be the perfect location for the next heist.

"There's nobody out there," Matt said. "You must be hearing things."

I'm hearing the cha-ching of dollar signs if I can get rid of you.

"Huh. I guess so. That's weird." *I got to say this without throwing up.* "I'd really like to see your bedroom. Saving the best for last, I bet."

His fat cheeks turned bright red and I could see

the front of his sweatpants poke out a bit. He hurried over to the doorway and motioned for me to come over.

Think of all the money. Think of all the money.

Chapter Eight

Think of Grant. Think of Grant. Trish thought as the murderer's penis thrust back and forth between her red lips. She pulled it out and swirled her tongue around the head. The giant of a man had proved himself to be just as big down there. She had hoped that she could get him off and he would let her live, but she had been going down on him for what seemed like forever. She'd have to resort to Plan B.

She let go of his penis, stood up, and hopped up on the desk. Devin gave her a strange look, but that quickly turned into a grin as Trish spread her legs wide and slid her hand down the front of her black panties. She faked a moan as best as she could and pushed her fingers against her barely wet vagina. She rubbed faster, hoping that it wouldn't betray her when she needed to use it.

"I can't take it anymore, Devin. You've got me so hot. Fuck me!" she yelled, as she reached up and pinched one of her nipples.

Devin stood between her legs with his dick in one hand and that bloody hammer in his other. Trish silently pleaded to God that he would choose his penis.

"I prefer doggy style. I'm a bit of an ass man."

The words surprised Trish at first. If he weren't holding onto that weapon and didn't have that scar across his head, he could almost pass for any red blooded male. She pulled her fingers out of her thong and put them into her mouth, sucking her juices off them. *It'll have to do.* Then, she turned over on the edge of the desk and pushed her ass up in the air.

"Ready when you are, lover boy."

Trish felt the head of his penis press against the fabric of her satin underwear. Again, she was trying to think of anyone other than him. Grant wasn't working. Maybe it was because he was dead in the next room. Her husband, Terry didn't do it for her anymore. She was trying to think of other sexy male co-workers when she felt the thin string between her ass cheeks get pulled up. She figured he'd pull them down, but maybe he liked to leave them on. She had slept with a few guys that were into that. Then, she felt the wet, hard end of hammer press against her tailbone. She looked back and saw that his tool was underneath the back of her thong.

Devin bent over her and grabbed a hold of her hair. He whispered in her ear, "Not only do I like it doggy style, but can you guess what else I like?"

Trish couldn't bring herself to speak. She could feel blood dripping off his hammer and running down her ass crack.

"Three-ways."

With that, he lifted her up by her hair and her underwear, painfully carrying her towards the door, back out to the living room, back to where Grant was.

Shaun Hupp

Chapter Nine

It sounded like I had just stepped in mud when I entered the room.

"Sorry," he said. "I had a little spill before you came and didn't have time to clean it up."

It was more than just the floor that needed cleaning up. The room smelled of grease and sweat. He probably never cleaned it and he probably never left his room. I had no doubt that his computer's browser history was probably full of porn and his hamper was full of crusty tube socks. I needed to get out of here as soon as possible

Let's get this over with.

I went over and sat on his bed. "So. . . This is where the magic happens, I take it?"

He looked at me like I was an alien and started stuttering. I let out the best fake giggle I could muster. I patted the spot next to me for him to sit. It felt oddly moist and I tried to disguise my disgust. He slowly made his way over to me and sat a good foot away from me.

I came out and said it: "Matt, are you a virgin?"

His red face drained of all its color. "Wha. . . What? Of course, not! I've slept with plenty of girls.

Maybe, ten or twelve for sure."

I laughed. I couldn't help it, but I recovered nicely. "You don't have to lie to me, Matt. I could tell."

He put his head down. "Okay. I'm a virgin."

I couldn't even look at him when I said, "Well. . . We could change that." I hoped he thought I was just shy, rather than hiding my look of repulsion.

"Really?"

I turned back to him and gave him that telltale smile that made every guy do what I wanted. "Really. Think of it as a 'thank you' for being such a Good Samaritan."

He smiled, probably close to exploding in those nasty sweatpants. "Okay. How do you want to get started? Do I just-"

"Lie down," I interrupted as I pointed to the head of the bed, "and I'll take care of everything."

He did as I asked. *Almost there*, I thought.

I climbed on top of him and immediately he let out a moan, even though I was pretty sure I was on his stomach. "Close your eyes and keep them closed."

He closed them. I took his two meaty hands and

place them on my breasts. *The things I'll do to make a quick buck,* I thought as he squeezed them roughly through my shirt. I reached down and pulled my set of handcuffs out of the front pocket of my shorts. I quietly hooked both opened ends to a bracelet I was wearing, pulled his hands away from my breasts, and slammed them behind his head, pressing my chest to his face. I was trying to block his view in case he decided to cheat and peek. He slobbered all over them while I slid the handcuff's chain around the headboard railing.

Here goes nothing.

I slid one cuff around his wrist. He didn't seem to notice as he continued with whatever the hell he was doing with his tongue. I went to close it. It didn't fit. It just pinched his skin. Suddenly, he flipped me over onto my back and wrapped his fingers around my throat. His eyes were wild, yet focused.

"YOU'RE ALL THE SAME! YOU'RE ALL THE SAME!"

Shaun Hupp

Chapter Ten

I was so excited. I couldn't believe this was happening to me. Leah was one of the hottest girls in school and she wanted to meet me in the park after dark. She told me she would have a tent set up for us since I couldn't sneak into her bedroom and she couldn't into mine.

I was skeptical at first. I was a skinny nerd and wasn't much to look at. We were both freshmen, but she could get any guy from any grade she wanted. We certainly didn't hang out in the same cliques. In fact, I'm pretty sure some of the other kids she hung out with picked on me; however, she swore up and down that she had always admired me from afar. I still wasn't too sure until she started sending me naked pictures of herself: boobs, ass, pussy, never the face though. I asked why and she said she still wasn't sure she could trust me yet. She didn't want her face ending up on the internet for the whole school to see. She wanted to trust me though. She wanted to get to know me. She wanted me.

It didn't take me long to find the bright orange tent and the gorgeous Leah lying with the front half her body outside the flap opening, illuminated by her cell phone. When she heard me approach, she looked frightened at first and then, relieved. "I was starting to worry you wouldn't show."

Trying to act cool, I said, "You shouldn't have worried.

She smiled and disappeared into the tent. I was confused at first and then, I saw a pair of lacy, pink panties fly out the opening. *Is this really happening?* I thought as I approached her underwear.

I was still out of sight from the flap so lifted them to my nose and inhaled. I wasn't sure what they would smell like. I was disappointed that they didn't really smell like anything. I dropped them back on the ground and went inside.

"Hi," she purred.

"Hi," I repeated back at her, awkwardly. *So much for acting cool.*

"Well. . . I showed you mine. . . Aren't you going to show me yours?"

She didn't have to tell me twice. My teenage hormones were in complete control as I stripped down to my tightie whities. Usually, I didn't like getting undressed in front of other people in the gym locker room, but I felt safe with Leah.

She looked like she approved of what she saw and she went to lift up her sweater. It barely went up a couple inches before she lowered it back down and a devious grin formed on her face.

"I have an idea. Hold on." With that, she turned around and peered into her backpack, giving me a great view of her ass through her short skirt. I swore I could see a panty line when she turned around. She had a long, black piece of cloth and a set of silver handcuffs.

She crawled back over to me and leaned forward with her lips puckered. I closed my eyes, preparing myself for my first kiss when I felt her hands on my bare chest. She pushed me down. My eyes shot open and I saw her scurry out of the tent.

"Catch me!"

I crawled towards the edge of the tent and saw her silhouette disappear behind a tree. I thought about putting my clothes back on, but that would probably upset her. I was scared of being seen, although I did not see anyone else in the park.

You only live once, I thought as I took off after her in just my underwear and socks.

I didn't find her; she found me. I was practically exhausted and I didn't hear her sneak up behind me. She quickly put what I realized was a blindfold over my eyes and whispered into my ear, "Shhhhh. . . Let me take care of you."

She took my hand and led me through the woods. After a while, she stopped and spun me around. "Lie on the ground and put your hands over your head. I want to suck your dick, Matt."

Again, I did just as she said with no hesitation, letting the leaves and grass scratch at my back and legs. I felt her place the cuffs around my wrists and heard them click. I pulled a little on them and felt them securely attached to what I assumed was a tree.

I sensed her standing over me and then, I heard it: the sound of dozens of feet walking and kicking through fallen leaves.

"Leah? What's going o-"

The blindfold was pulled away and I was staring up at a group of kids from my school. As my eyes scanned each face, I saw guys and girls that hurled insults at me during the day. Some of the guys even physically shoved me around. Then, my eyes rested on him: Tony Miller. He was the worst of them all.

"Hey, dork! Did you think you were going to get lucky tonight?"

I yelled out, hoping someone nearby might hear

and help me. The others looked around nervously, but Tony wasn't fazed. He nudged the guy next to him and said something in his ear. The guy, John knelt down and pulled my underwear down. I stopped screaming and the group started laughing at me. I went to scream again. John wadded up my briefs and stuck them in my mouth. I gagged as I tasted what was either sweat or piss.

"Gross," said one of the nameless guys. "That had a skidmark on it."

I continued to cough and gag when Leah leaned over me. "This is for checking out my ass non-stop for the past two or three years. You're such a pervert and I hope this teaches you a lesson."

I finally manage to spit my underwear out of my mouth. "Please, I'm sorry. I'll never do it again. I swear."

"It's too late for sorries," she said. "Someone like you is never going to get someone like me. I mean, look at you and look at me. And clearly, you aren't packing anything down there either."

"Please," I cried. "Just let me go."

"Oh, we're not done with you," Tony said, as he pulled out his cell phone. Then, they all pulled out their phones and the forest was illuminated by the flashes from their phones. "Now, everyone in the whole school is going to see your tiny dick. Better get used to jacking off because you ain't ever going to get laid."

I felt teardrops streaming down the side of my head, and then I felt other drops all over my naked body. Confused at first, then I realized: *rain.* It was then that I heard the clap of thunder overhead. Quickly, the few drops turned into a hard, constant down pouring. My tormentors fled in different directions leaving me all alone. I resumed my screaming, spitting out water every so often. I pulled at handcuffs, but it was no use.

It seemed like I was yelling for hours all the while, the storm raged on, drowning me out. I tried climbing up the tree, but the cuffs got in the way when I got to the branches. I finally gave up, laid back down in the mud, turned my head to the side, and, through the rain, saw a figure approaching.

"Help me!" I begged. "Please! I need help!" I blinked my eyes, trying desperately to see through the heavy rainfall.

Blink. The figure continued passed a tree.

Blink. The figure stepped over a log.

Blink. The figure was gone.

I couldn't comprehend what my eyes had seen. I started screaming for him or her to come back. I pulled at my shackles, but it was no use. Exhausted, shivering from the cold, I shut my eyes and began to cry again.

"What's the matter, you anorexic fuck? Afraid of a little rain?"

I opened my eyes and saw Tony crouching beside me. I kicked at him, but he easily avoided it.

"Easy, dweeb. I just came here to keep you company."

"LET ME GO!"

"No can do. I don't have the keys, but I'm sure someone will come along after this storm dies down that can help, you know, in the morning most likely."

"Why are you doing this to me!?" I cried as lightning flashed overhead.

"I'm not doing anything to you. I just thought we could talk."

And we did just that or at least, he did. The storm continued and so did his taunts. Finally, when the sun came up, a jogger spotted me and called the police on his cell phone. An officer arrived five minutes later.

"Hold on, son. I'll get you out shortly," he said, as he put a blanket over my naked body. "These sorts of handcuffs always have the same keys. I have a master set and one of them should pop them open. Then, I'll take you back to the station and you can tell me who did this to you."

"It was him." I looked at Tony.

"Him, who?" the officer asked, looking in the direction I was.

"Don't you. . ." Tony smiled and it dawned on me that he wasn't really there. This 'Tony' wasn't the same Tony that tricked me. This one only I could see.

"Nevermind. I'm sorry, officer. I've had a long night."

He nodded and after several tries, found the right key. With the cuffs off, he had me put my underwear back on. I kept the blanket over me as he took me to his squad car. He said he'd send another unit to the park to look for Leah's tent and my clothes while he took me to the station. I got in the back and Tony was already inside.

"You think if you asked him real nice, he'd stop off for some fast food. You're skin and bones, Matty. You should really eat something."

Chapter Eleven

"Put it in your mouth."

Devin knelt beside her and held Trish by her hair. He shoved her face against Grant's flaccid penis. She used to love to do this, but that was when Grant was alive. It didn't help that his bowels had released upon his death. The stench of piss, shit, and blood filled the room, but the source was directly underneath him and right below her nose.

"DO IT!" Devin yelled, as he took her chin in his hand and pressed her lips to the head of Grant's penis.

Trish silently wished that Grant was a grower and not a shower. She took his soft penis with her hand and guided it into her mouth. She gagged, but not in the usual way. It reminded her of her college days when they had a hot dog blowjob contest at her sorority.

Except this hot dog was attached to a dead body.

"Suck it good, whore. Maybe rigor mortis will set in and he'll get a hard-on for you," Devin said, as he stood up and got behind her. He pulled her thong down and grunted as he attempted to push himself into Trish. There was nothing she could do to find any sort of arousal. Regardless, he managed to get himself deep inside and started painfully thrusting.

Please. . . Just kill me, Trish thought as she tried not to throw up.

His thrusts intensified. She was bone dry, but he didn't seem to notice or if he noticed, he didn't care. He moaned. Trish cried.

"Quit your cryin', girlie," he said, slapping her ass between thrusts. "It's downright shameful. I thought you wanted to have some fun!"

She couldn't stop herself. The pain between her legs, the rancid smell of feces, and the limp and lifeless penis between her lips created a perfect storm of tears. She tried to block it all out. She had heard about how some rape victims were able to mentally take themselves some place while they were being violated. She tried to think about something else, somewhere else.

She didn't think it was working, and then, suddenly, it must have. She was no longer lying down on a cold corpse, but on the hot sands of a beach in Hawaii where she and Terry had vacationed several years ago. The smell of the ocean air had replaced the foul smell of shit. The sounds of grunts and moans had changed into the sounds of crashing waves.

She looked over and saw Terry passed out on a

blanket next to her. Despite the little bit of drool coming out the side of his mouth, he looked good. This was how she remembered him before his promotion. He still had a full head of hair and she couldn't see any grays. He seemed so stress-free, even though they could barely afford this trip.   Trish reached and poked his slight paunch of a belly.

"Hey! I'm awake! I'm awake. I swear I didn't fall asleep."

"Sure. You didn't," Trish teased.

"Okay, I fell asleep," Terry said, coming clean. "That time change is really kicking my ass. I'm sorry. Were you saying something?"

"No. I just wanted to tell you that I love you."

"You woke me up just to tell me that? I'm going back to sleep," he joked.

"No, you jerk! I had something else to say to you."

"Is it related to how buff and handsome I look in my new swim trunks?"

"No. I mean, you do, but that's not it. Be serious, Terry. Please."

His smile went away. "Sure, Trish. Sorry. What

is it?"

"Terry, promise me that what we have together won't change. Promise me that you'll say no to a high-paying promotion with long hours. I need you, Terry. I don't care about having a big house or lots of fancy things. I just want you."

He looked confused. "But Trish, Mr. Hayes is retiring soon and he said he wants me to take over his position in the company. I know I might have to work a little bit more, but the pay is-"

"No," Trish said as a tear rolled down her cheek. "Please, Terry. It's not worth it. We don't need all that money. Promise me."

He reached over and wiped the tears from her eyes. "You mean more to me than some stupid promotion. I just want you to be happy and if that's what it takes, then I prom-"

The hammer slammed down on the back of Trish's head. Her jaws clamped shut, tearing through flesh and muscle, filling her mouth with an orgasm of blood. Devin threw her off the sofa onto her back. A trail of semen leaked out her vagina.

The pain in the back of her head was excruciating, but Trish was more concerned about her throat. The lubricated, severed penis had slid down her trachea. She gagged and choked. She clawed at her neck, leaving bloody scratch marks. She felt woozy, unsure if it was because of the lack of oxygen or her head wound. Her vision blurred as Devin crouched over her body.

"Girl can't even deep throat. Shameful."

Shaun Hupp

Chapter Twelve

Her eyes bulged as my hands tightened around her throat. She dug her fingernails into my wrists. I felt nothing even after I saw the blood dripping onto the sheet of my bed.

"I didn't think you had it in you, Fatty Matty."

I looked over at Tony and screamed, "Shut up! Don't call me that!"

"I don't understand why you are even using those chubby hands. Just smother her with that belly."

"SHUT UP! You're not real. You're not real!" I yelled, as Nikki clawed and slapped at my face.

"You're a real piece of work, fat fuck. You finally get a girl in bed, you get to play with her titties, and now, you're trying to kill her? And why? All because of what we did to you a few years ago?"

He was right. What was I doing?

I let go of Nikki and climbed off her. She gasped and started coughing. I got off the bed to give her some space. Tony hopped up on the bed next to her and rested his hands behind his head.

"You better apologize, tubby. Best you can hope

for now is a handjob."

"I'm sorry, Nikki. . . I don't know what came over me."

She coughed some more and then, finally said, "You're sorry? You're sorry!?"

"Oh, boy. She seems pissed, Matty. Maybe apologizing isn't going to cut it. Maybe you should take her out to dinner. You know, somewhere fancy with numbered value meals. You order numbers one through nine and she can have a number ten."

Ignore him.

I cautiously approached Nikki, but she scrambled off the bed, putting it, and Tony, between us. She reached into her front jean pocket and pulled out a switchblade. She looked around for a way out, but her back was against the wall and the doorway was behind me.

"Stay the hell away from me," she threatened as she pointed the tip at me.

Tony looked up at his reflection in the trembling blade and smoothed his perfect hair. "If you whip out a fork, I'll know it was meant to be."

"Look," I said as calmly as I could. "I didn't mean

to do that. Just put down the knife and let me explain."

"No! You listen to me. You're going to get out of my way. I'm leaving."

Tony stopped admiring himself and looked up at me. "You know, if she leaves here, she'll go to the cops, right? How do you think this will look to them?"

"Shut up!" I yelled at Tony.

Nikki thrust the knife at me. "No. You shut up. I'm leaving, you fat fuck!"

I stood silently in shock. Tony laughed. "Aww, that's so cute. She used my pet name for you. A woman after my own heart."

Before I knew what was happening, I rushed to the edge of the bed, grabbed the side of the bed frame, lifted it up, and slammed Tony and Nikki against the wall. Nikki screamed out as her body struck the wall. I pressed my stomach against the bottom and held it in place. I looked up and realized my face was only a few inches from hers, but she posed no risk since her arms were pinned between the wall and the queen-size mattress.

Tony, however, was not. I felt him behind me with his mouth next to my ear. "Now's your chance. You can have your first kiss. She's helpless."

I didn't say anything. I stared at Nikki as she continued to struggle. I shook my head.

"I know it seems wrong, Matt, but look at what she's put you through. One tiny kiss is the least she could give you for all the pain she caused. She's a guest in your house. You're in charge."

He's right. I'm in charge.

I leaned in and planted one on her. Within seconds, I felt her teeth bite down on my bottom lip. I tried to pull away, but it was no use. Nikki shook her head like a dog with a chew toy until my lower lip tore from my face.

I screamed out, stumbling backward. Tony pointed and yelled, "The bed!"

Nikki managed to push the mattress away from the wall, but not far enough. I slammed my body against the frame again, smashing her head against the wall. I held it there, trying to decide what to do. Nikki stared at me, her face full of rage, and then, spit the bloody piece of flesh at me.

I wiped my face against the shoulder of my T-shirt. The exposed flesh where my lip had been rubbed against the fabric sending screaming waves of pain to my head. I wanted to curl up into a ball and cry, but I held onto the bed frame.

"Are you going to take that, Matty?" Tony asked in my ear as Nikki stared. She gave me that perfect smile, letting me see the blood on her formerly white teeth. "She deserves to be taught a lesson for what she did to you."

He's right. I was nothing but nice to this bitch and look what she did to me.

"Exactly. You know what they say; an eye for an eye, a lip for a lip."

I smiled back at Nikki. She looked horrified. I could only imagine what my face looked like. I dove at her teeth first and latched onto her cheek. I was aiming for her lips, but she turned her head at the last second. I didn't care. I chomped down as hard as I could, pretending it was a very rare steak. She screamed as the skin peeled away. I let the strip of flesh hit the floor and I went back for seconds. This time my extra large mouth managed to get both sets of her lips. *Bull's eye,* I thought as I ripped them off her face and spit them out onto the floor.

"Keep going, Matty! Make her pay. Keep going

and super-size your meal."

And I did just that. I couldn't stop. My teeth tore chunk after chunk while Tony cheered on the sidelines. I must have blacked out, losing track of time. When I finally regained my sense of awareness, I looked at what was left of Nikki. She wouldn't ever be able to hide that perfect smile because there was simply nothing to cover it with.

Her perfect features were gone, as was much of her skin and the muscles of her face. Patches of bloody bone could be seen where I had taken out large hunks of meat. I must have torn off both ears and her nose. If it weren't for her teeth and glazed over eyes, you would have never known this was a human head.

When it dawned on me what I had done, I backed away from the bed. It and Nikki's limp body fell forward. The frame crashed down on the floor. Nikki's body lay lifeless, thankfully facing down with her hair covering most of the damage. The sheets were soaked in blood and gore. Pounds of flesh littered the carpet.

Tony laughed. "This is a little worse than a spilled soda. I think your parents will notice."

I turned and looked at myself in the mirror. My body still didn't fit the frame, but that's not what caught my attention. My clothes literally dripped with blood. I leaned forward and examined my ruined face. Before all this, I never would have said I had the looks of a leading man of Hollywood. Now, I looked like something straight out of a horror movie.

I continued to stare, not believing what I was seeing until the sound of footsteps broke my concentration. I looked over at Tony, but he was sitting on the blood-spattered mattress. He shrugged his shoulders. It was then that I realized the sound was coming up the stairs.

My parents, I thought. *How do I explain this?*

Chapter Thirteen

I stared down at the woman as the life left her eyes. *Such a waste*, I thought as I tucked my penis back into my pants. *I guess my sort of lifestyle doesn't really jive well with having a long term relationship.*

The sound of footsteps coming from the kitchen grabbed my attention. I gripped my hammer tight and waited to see who came through the door. It could have been a neighbor or maybe the police if I somehow missed a silent alarm. The door swung open and a familiar face stepped forward.

"Aww, shit, Devin! Seriously? This is one of the reasons why I didn't want to work with you."

My sister, Nikki walked over to the body on the floor and then, noticed the body on the couch. She stormed off and vanished back into the kitchen. *Shit.* I chased after her.

"Nikki, please! It just sort of happened."

She stopped and spun around in front of the refrigerator. "When I agreed to work with you, I didn't think it would be like this. I'm not. . . into all that."

I reached out to take her hand, but she moved back. Then, I felt stupid when I saw the blood on my palm. *I loved my sister with all my heart, but I had these urges. I couldn't control myself sometimes. She couldn't accept who I was.*

"I'm sorry, Nikki but you told me no one was going to be home," I explained, finally standing my ground. "That's your fault."

"My fault? It's my fault there are two dead bodies in the other room and one is missing his dick!"

"Yes, it's your fault. You're supposed to be the one 'researching' these locations. I'm the one that does all the dirty work. It's just that this time. . . I got dirtier than usual."

Nikki stared me down, but I wasn't flinching this time. I'm the older brother. I'm the one that mom told her to listen to before she died; Not that she ever listened to mom. She wasn't going to win this argument.

"Fine, Devin. Fine. You know what? Let's get whatever valuables we can find and get out of here. You know the police will be putting all their manpower into finding whoever did this. If it were just a simple burglary, they'd barely bat an eye. It looks like you left plenty of DNA for them to go off of too."

I shook my head. "Not after I torch the place. I always have a plan, sis. It's shameful for you to think I wouldn't."

"Fine. Burn this fucker down, but next time, things are going to be different. I've been scouting a place for a while. It's in the middle of nowhere, the guy owns a bunch of factories, and the family always goes out for hours Saturday afternoon."

"As long as no one is home, I'll be on my best behavior."

"No. I told you, Devin: things are going to be different. I'm going to be the one to go in."

"Then, what am I going to do?"

"It's, as you would say, shameful for you to think I don't have a plan. We'll both go to the location as usual, but instead of me being the lookout. You'll be doing that. I'll call you when I need your help with the loot. If I don't call you in like thirty minutes after I go in, then you can use your big macho hammer and come rescue me. Deal?"

I didn't like it. My baby sister could be walking into all sorts of dangerous situations, but I also knew that she knew how to handle herself. She was tough. It ran in the family. And as pissed as she was, I didn't have much of a choice but to trust her.

"Deal."

Chapter Fourteen

A man appeared in the doorway. He wore camo head-to-toe, which was a lot of camo because this guy was huge. It was then that I noticed the giant hammer in his right hand. I didn't know what he wanted, but it couldn't be good.

"Where's Nikki?"

I realized that even with his great height, he still couldn't see behind my fat frame. I thought about trying to lie to him, but with my clothes, skin, and hair drenched in blood, I didn't think he'd believe whatever I told him. I quickly turned and ran around the bed, putting it between us.

"Nikki!" he yelled, as he rushed over to her face-down body. The man put his weapon on the bloody mattress and knelt down. He cautiously brushed the hair away from her face and when he lifted her head, he gasped and fell backward. Tony appeared behind him.

"Oh, shit, Fatty Matty. I think you're in serious trouble."

If the man hadn't fallen in front of the door, I would have made a break for it. He didn't seem to be even paying attention to me anymore. He looked to be in shock so I knew I had to act fast. I considered going for the window, but I'd have to crawl on top of the bed and it was difficult to open. Not to mention the second story drop. I looked for other options and that's when I saw Nikki's switchblade on the carpet by my foot. I checked to make sure he was still on the ground. I crouched down hoping the man wouldn't notice, grabbed the knife, and when I stood up, he was also standing.

"You killed her," he said, as he picked his hammer back up.

"Here we go!" Tony clapped with excitement. "It's about to go down."

I held up my hands. "No, no, no! She attacked me and-"I realized he was staring at the knife in my hand. *Shit.*

I ran for it, but in two big strides, he was on me. I slashed at him and he easily grabbed my wrist. He slammed it down my dresser, but I didn't let go of it. It was my only weapon, my only hope. He lifted my arm up and slammed it down again. Somehow I managed to hold on. Then, he held my wrist down with his left hand and raised the hammer over his head. He smiled as he brought the hammer down. But instead of hitting my hand, he struck the blade. Releasing his grip, I fell backward. He ignored me and stared at the switchblade.

Then, he smashed his hammer into it over and over again, sending wooden shrapnel in every direction. I covered my face and eyes with my hands, and when I finally thought it was safe, I peeked between my fat fingers. He just stood there, admiring what he had done to the bent and broken blade in his hand.

Suddenly, he threw the knife to the side and rushed at me. I covered myself, preparing for the worst, but he just stopped and crouched down in front of me. "This scar," he pointed to his forehead. "That knife did that. SHE did that. All my life, I protected her. I guess you could say I was the typical big brother in that sense, but I knew something about me was different. I made the mistake of telling a school counselor about my unique urges and she suggested that I join the Army. It would let me act on those urges and hopefully, straighten me out. I gave Nikki that very knife for protection and left the next day to fight for Uncle Sam. When I came back, I had learned that that knife was useless when she was attacked by a group of five men. They gang raped her and left her for dead. She survived and when I came back, I didn't get a hero's welcome and it wasn't a warm embrace I received upon my arrival. It was this scar. She blamed me. The family blamed me. I blamed me. From then on, I swore to her and everybody else that I'd never let anything happen to her ever again, but at the same time, I knew that something inside of her had changed.

She wasn't the same defenseless, little girl I had left. There was something dark hiding within her that had come out. I saw the darkness in myself reflected in her."

He stood up and walked over to Nikki's corpse. Then, he raised his hammer high and brought it down over and over again on the back of her head. Her skull collapsed inward with each blow and instead of wood fragments coming my way, I had blood, bone, and brain matter. I looked away again. When I looked back, there was nothing left but a neck stump and a pile of gore. Even Tony looked speechless.

"Before our mom died, she made me promise that I'd protect her for the rest of my life, no matter what. I could never break that promise, even though I wanted to so bad. She treated me like shit. She didn't understand my urges. Now, because of you, I'm free. I don't have to do these silly burglaries anymore. I can be exactly the kind of person I always wanted to be. No more holding back. The leash is off."

He turned and stared at me. "Thank you."

"You're. . . welcome," I barely managed to spit out.

"It's a shame I still have to kill you."

My heart stopped, my lungs emptied, Tony

laughed. I thought I was free. I thought I had done this great thing for him and he was going to go on his merry way.

"It's nothing personal, but if I've learned one thing from my sister, it's how to avoid getting caught and with that, eliminating loose ends. YOU are a loose end."

He walked over to me and I burst into tears. It wasn't fair.

"I'm sorry, kid. It has to be this way. Just put your head down and I promise I'll do this as quickly as possible."

I lowered my head and I felt the top of the hammer pressed against it. *This is it.* I looked over and saw Tony. He was grinning ear-to-ear.

"Any last requests? You've earned it, kid."

I couldn't think of anything and then, I saw my closet. "Yeah. . . I have one. My grandfather was in the military. Before he died, he gave me the medals he earned in combat. I always kept them in that closet because I was ashamed that I wasn't the man my grandfather had hoped I'd become. I was hoping you'd let me wear them when. . . when you kill me. Maybe that way I'll die as a man somewhat. I don't know. I guess it sounds stupid when you say it out loud."

I sat there, waiting. Finally, I felt the hammer come away from the back of my head. "No. It's not stupid," he said. "Go get them."

I looked up at him and nodded. I slowly rose and walked to the closet. Tony gave me a weird look. "You never met your grandfather. What are you up to? What do you have in that closet anyway?"

I opened the closet door and reached inside. When I found what I was searching for, I grabbed it and pulled it out. I turned back to the man and his eyes went wide. I raised the LAR-47 assault rifle to my shoulder and pulled the trigger. Bullets burst forth, throwing me back into the closet. I had never shot the thing before and wasn't expecting that. Despite my inexperience, I couldn't miss at this distance. As I continued firing until the magazine was empty, the man's body danced with each hit until he finally fell onto the bed, next to Nikki.

I looked over at the inside of the closet door. There I had pages of my yearbook tacked. There were red circles around pictures and names; people like Leah, John, Tony, and all the others. There was a map of the school normally reserved for marking fire exits. This version marked where each student would be during second hour.

"You were going to kill me," Tony said, as he stood

in front of the carnage. Somehow my subconscious version of him was as oblivious to my plans as the real one. "You were going to kill all of us."

"Monday," I said, out of breath. "Monday, it would have been all over."

Tony stood there in shock and slowly, a smile crept up on his face. "But not anymore."

"What?" I didn't understand.

"Don't you see, fat fuck? It's over. There won't be any class for you on Monday. Even if you somehow managed to clean all this up and hide it from your parents, your messed up face will give you away." He laughed. "Do you get it now? I win. I WIN!"

I threw the now useless gun down and reach behind me. I grabbed the Mossberg 500 shotgun. I aimed and emptied it at Tony. Every bullet just went right through him while he pointed and laughed me. I tossed it aside and grabbed one of my handguns. I took aim but realized it was useless.

I had been planning my revenge for a while. I managed to sneak the guns out of my uncle's house. He had quite the collection and would have never noticed them missing. All the ammunition came from different locations. I had been slowly stockpiling it.

Tony walked over to me and knelt down. "I know what you're thinking. You're thinking you could kill your parents and then, nothing will stop you until Monday. Wrong. You're not that far out in the boonies. You don't think your neighbors heard all that shooting? Hell, you probably gave Mr. Myers a heart attack. The police will be here soon, fat fuck. It's over."

Ignore him. You can fix this. You can run away and hide until Monday.

I crawled forward, still with the gun in my hand. I didn't want to see the mutilated corpses on my bed. Tony appeared next to me, yelling in my ear. "You can't run, Fatty Matty. When the police show up, they'll see your plans. They'll search everywhere. The school will be closed until you're found. It's over!"

I stopped crawling. Now, Tony was directly in front of me. "You know I'm right. And guess what? When the police arrest you, you'll be put away forever. Think about it. No more porn. No more fast food. Just a small, gray cell. Just you and me for the rest of your life."

"No."

"Yes," Tony said in my right ear. I looked over and he was there, but he was also in front of me. He had never appeared to me before in multiple versions of himself.

"You know what you have to do," a new Tony on my left said. "You need to finally end it."

"No."

"You don't want to share a cell with me, do you?" asked the Tony in front of me. "Just do it. There are no other options."

"Kill yourself," the two Tonys on either side of me said in unison.

"No."

The Tony in front said, "I can hear the sirens in the distance. You need to act quickly."

"Kill yourself," they yelled.

"I can't do it."

"Yes, you can. Just put the barrel of that gun in your mouth and pull the trigger."

"Kill yourself!"

"Please, just leave me alone. I can't think."

"They'll be pulling up soon. They'll surround the house. There will be nowhere you can go. You have to do this now!"

"Kill yourself!"

I sat down and slowly raised the gun to my mouth. I closed my eyes and put the barrel in my mouth.

"It'll be over in an instant. Just pull the trigger and all the pain will go away."

"Kill yourself!"

My finger found the trigger.

"I won."

I pulled it.

The cane dropped from Emrys's hand. Luke shook off his hypnosis, knocking candies out of his hair. Emrys was barely breathing, but the story was finished. There were just a couple more things that needed to be done. He reached into his impossibly deep coat and pulled out yet another antique box.

"This is for you, son. It's going to help you save my life."

He handed it to him and then, reached down to get his cane. He felt dizzy. He knew he not only had to act fast, but he had to put himself in the middle of the action to absorb everything. After retrieving his cane, he carefully stood up and walked back the way he came. The group of teens was still joking around when Emrys put himself between them and Luke.

"Hey! Get out of the way, old man."

"Yeah. We were just trying to give him some candy. As soon as we get off at our stop, you know he's going to crawl on the floor and eat every one of those."

"ENOUGH!"

Emrys's bellow took more out of him than he anticipated. He collapsed on the floor. Not one of the teens moved to help him. They just laughed at him. Emrys's eye was inches away from the globe. The red at the bottom was nothing more than a pinprick. He grabbed the sphere, raised it a couple of inches off the ground, and tapped it twice on the floor of the train car.

His knocking awakened the very seed he had planted in Luke with his story. Luke rose from his seat and faced the group. A blank expression never left his face as he opened the old box and pulled out two handguns.

The teens screams were soon drowned out by the echoing shots as Luke opened fire at his tormentors. He wasn't a great marksman. They tried to hide behind the seats, but with every shot, Emrys was able to help Luke's aim little by little. Soon, the screams died down and blood spilled out into the aisle way, creeping towards Emrys. He reached out his cane and smeared red all over the globe. He felt a surge of energy throughout his body. His bones and muscles strengthened, allowing him to stand. Luke was still firing at his now deceased bullies. Emrys was still in the middle of the shooting, but he was now completely in control of the environment. No bullet would touch him if he didn't allow it. The gunmetal grey projectiles flew past his head just as the grey of his hair started to recede, leaving behind its original jet black color.

Both guns were empty. Luke suddenly dropped the weapons on the floor and rushed away from Emrys.

The box that had been on the floor had vanished.

"What did I do!? How did you make me do that!? What are you? Stay away from me!"

Emrys smiled, wrinkles that were there previously were now gone, his teeth not so yellow anymore. "What did I do? I gave you the ability to do what you wanted. You beat your bullies. How did I make you do that? The power of suggestion is at my disposal, my dear boy. I just gave you the push needed. You did that. What am I? I doubt very much you would understand."

Luke was shaking on the ground. He didn't say anything.

"You're welcome. The youth these days can't even thank someone for their help." Emrys shook his head, turned, and walked out the door.

The next couple of cars were still empty. Emrys finally reached a car he knew was full. He entered and was surprised to find most of the people standing near the door.

"Hey! We thought we heard some gunshots. Is everything okay?" The man held a camera phone in his hand, no doubt waiting to capture anything to post on Facebook to get likes and shares. He had dreams of being a viral star. Emrys could help him.

"Everything is just fine," Emrys said, searching for the reader, the daughter. When he saw her with her nose still in her book, he gave the bottom of his cane two gentle taps.

They didn't even notice her stand up. From the box, she pulled out a surgical scalpel. The box dropped from her hand but disappeared before it could hit the floor. One of the men in back screamed out first, dropping his iPad on the ground. The others turned to see what had happened and the reader slashed a woman's throat. She desperately held onto her neck, trying to stop the bleeding, but her iPod and body ended up falling into a pool of her own blood. The rest of the passengers attempted to leave from the door Emrys had just come from. Emrys used his abilities to lock it, for the red of his cane was slowly growing. The next man caught the scalpel in his eye. He screamed as the reader twisted, carving it out like a hole in a jack-o-lantern. The rest were pinned to the wall as she continued her assault, methodically killing one after another.

Blood flew freely in the air as Emrys embraced its mist, pushing through the crowd of soon to be corpses. More wrinkles disappeared, his teeth turned pearly white. This had been going better than he had planned and there was so much more behind the next door.

The next car had the racist, his son, and the teens.

Emrys had enough power to change his appearance, but he decided not to. The other teens had treated him harshly and he wanted to see what this group would do when he walked in covered in blood.

"Holy shit! Are you okay man?"

Emrys was surprised. All of the teenagers came forward to check on him. It was a nice gesture, but they were going to be helpful in a much different way.

Tap. Tap.

They didn't notice as the father stood up, hammer in hand, and came up behind them. His child remained asleep until the first hammer strike. The teens' screaming woke him and he joined in screaming as he watched his father bash in their skulls. The boys tried to fight back, but the floor was slick with blood, causing them to fall down. Emrys had designed it that way.

The father continued breaking bones while Emrys made his way over to the child. The boy was cowering behind a seat. "Don't worry, child. Remember, your father is doing this for you."

With that, Emrys walked, unaided by his cane to the door. The handle turned without him touching it and he entered the final car. He decided to camouflage his blood stained clothes.

Back to where I started.

Marianna and Ryan were still sitting in the front sleeping and Marianna's mother, Joan was still towards the middle. She looked sad. It was as if nothing had changed, but Emrys would take care of that.

Tap. Tap.

Joan stood up and opened her box, revealing a nail file inside. She silently walked to the front with no one paying attention to her. She bent over Ryan and thrust the file into this exposed neck. He let out a small, gurgled cry. It was enough to wake Marianne.

"WHAT THE FUCK ARE YOU DOING!?"

Ryan fell to the floor, clutching his throat while blood poured out between his fingers. Joan held him down and repeatedly stabbed him in the chest and stomach. Marianne made a grab for her mother and caught an elbow to the face. She fell into the aisle way and look towards the rest of the train car.

"Help him! Someone! Please!"

Everyone in the car remained in their seats. No one moved to help him. They just continued on doing whatever they had been doing as if there wasn't someone being brutally slaughtered in front of them.

Some blood sprayed across the face of an old woman near them. She continued knitting as if nothing had happened.

"What is wrong with you people!? She's killing him!"

Marianne turned back to her mother to try to stop her, but it was too late. Joan was already standing with the crumpled body of Ryan underneath her. She was covered in blood and grinning ear-to-ear as if she had done something she had wanted to do for a long time.

"What is wrong with you!? You killed Ryan!"

Joan just stood there and said nothing. Emrys stepped between them. The top of cane swirled and glowed bright red. "Joan and Marianne, mother and daughter. . . That is a bond that should not be broken. I thank you two for finally making me whole again. How about you two go back to your seats and forget this ever happened? Marianne, you'll forget all about Ryan. You'll do what your mother asks of you. You two will love each other as a mother and daughter should. This is my gift to you both."

The two walked away from Emrys and went back to their seats. No one would find Ryan's body until the morning along with all the other carnage. The blood all over Joan would not be seen by anyone and his magic would continue on until the clothes were loaded into the washing machine and she showered. No one would remember Emrys. No video camera would capture his image. He had the power to do this now that he was strong enough.

He walked back to his seat and sat, looking back at his reflection in the glass. His body was back to being that of a man in his early twenties. He was perfection though he liked to remain average so that he could go unnoticed while feeding. He had enough energy to last quite awhile and his stop was coming up. He could just sit back and enjoy the rest of what was left of the night. Emrys could sense it was near midnight. He had thought today might have finally been the day he died. But, as it turned out, today had been a very good day. . . For him, anyway.

Thanks for reading. I hope you enjoyed it.

If I could ask my readers for one thing, it would

be to leave a review on Amazon and/or use social

media to tell others about my books.

It does a lot to support indie authors like myself.

Shaun Hupp

Shaun Hupp is a Michigan-based horror author who specializes in short stories and novelettes that range from supernatural thrillers to extreme horror. He can be found in several anthologies, but mainly likes to publish stories on his own quickly to satisfy his growing fanbase. His writing is heavily influenced by two guys named Richard: Laymon and Matheson.

You can head on over to his facebook page for info on new releases, upcoming projects, and other random craziness:

https://www.facebook.com/AuthorShaunHupp

Shaun Hupp

Printed in Great Britain
by Amazon

61141649R00129